THE ENEMY SEAS

THE
ENEMY SEAS

by
Gordon D. Shirreffs

THE WESTMINSTER PRESS
Philadelphia

LIBRARY OF CONGRESS CATALOG CARD NO. 65–17357

PUBLISHED BY THE WESTMINSTER PRESS®

PHILADELPHIA, PENNSYLVANIA

PRINTED IN THE UNITED STATES OF AMERICA

To the officers and men of *Harder* and *Wahoo,*
two submarines lost in action in World War II.
This story is essentially theirs.

1

LOGIE was making heavy weather of it through the howling murk that drove at her from dead ahead. The big *Fletcher*-class destroyer had hurled her twenty-one-hundred tons of steel almost too long into the face of the shrieking madness of the storm. Now she had been throttled down to take the smashing seas more easily, for she could not carry through her mission in this maelstrom of wind and water. She could develop 60,000-shaft horsepower to drive herself at 35 knots if she had to, but she *had* to slow down, pitching, heaving, and rolling like a thing gone mad, so she would not smash herself against the liquid fury of the storm that had howled down from the low latitudes of the North Pacific to turn northwest and then northeast. This buster of a storm had carried clear down to strike with vicious force between the Marshalls and the Carolines, as though fully aware that the U.S.S *Logie* was on duty off Kusaie Island looking for a downed reconnaissance plane.

Logie would have been in better condition to face the storm if she had not suffered artillery damage from Japanese shore batteries while doing close-in gun support to the Marines who had landed on Kwajalein. Her holed hull had been patched and well shored, good enough to take her safely to Brisbane for a refit, but Commander

Roberts, skipper of the *Logie,* had not anticipated being diverted from his course to Brisbane to look for the downed plane.

Logie shuddered and shook, pitched, rolled, and gyrated, burying her knifelike prow into the solid seas, hurling spray back against the superstructure like lead shot. Now and then errie sheet lightning flickered through the overhead murk and revealed the tumbling seas surging along in high waves with long, overhanging crests. The surface of the sea had a white appearance and the rolling of the waves was heavy and shocklike. To an old salt, this was Force 10 on the Beaufort Scale of Wind Force, indicating winds of 48 to 55 miles per hour statute. The common name for this madness of wind and water was a Whole Gale, and if one was to doubt this, all he had to do was ask any member of the *Logie's* crew about it. Another thing: the wind was steadily rising while the barometer was dropping. It looked as if an interesting night was coming on.

Signalman Second Class Bob Dunbar braced himself in his bunk with his life jacket and steel helmet, hooking an arm around a bunk stanchion just as *Logie* pitched deep, as though she was never coming up again. Bob rose gently from his bunk and literally flew across the space between his bunk and the next one to land heavily atop a cowering, lanky figure named Gary Lunt, Gunner's Mate Third Class. Before Gary could protest, the next heaving of the tin can lifted them together out of Gary's bunk and slammed them down on the steel deck, where they rolled down the steeply slanting surface to end up in a corner in a tangle of arms, legs, blankets, life jackets, books, pillows, and other assorted odds and ends that had long ago come adrift.

They untangled themselves and clawed their way up the deck, seemed to hang in a sort of limbo for a moment or two as *Logie* tried to figure out how to take on the next graybeard of a wave, and then they pitched downhill to end up against a bulkhead, finding Andy Sproul, Machinist's Mate Third Class, beneath them. When they saw the boy's face, they hauled him back to his bunk. " Lemme die," he croaked. "Lemme die! " They missed his next words as they tumbled into Bob's bunk, seemingly pressed against the bulkhead behind it by irresistible force.

Gary wiped the blood from his swollen nose.

Bob examined a skinned elbow. " We'd be better off on watch," he said.

Gary nodded. " She's buttoned up so tight down here the air is turning blue."

The ventilating fans were turning at top speed, but the howling wind topside was driving the foul air right back into the buttoned-up hull of the destroyer. With the foul air, the heat, and the green sickness of some of the crew, it seemed as though the thick atmosphere could raise the paint on the bulkheads.

A gigantic wave smashed against the portside of the destroyer and something snapped like a cannon shot. A dozen pairs of eyes looked upward as though at a command. " What was *that?* " Mike Rourke questioned.

" Breaking steel," said Gary.

" Yeah, but *what?* " said Carl Slater.

Gary yawned. " Probably lost the whole bridge," he said. " They don't make these old destroyers like they used to."

The speaker on the bulkhead rasped. " Now hear this! Now hear this! We've suffered heavy damage topside. The port bulwark on the main deck has been crushed. Two main stanchions supporting the bridge catwalk have snapped loose. Some oil drums have broken away aft and the motor whaler rolled completely under, snapping the griping spar and jumping its releasing gear. We need volunteers to secure it. Report to Chief West aft of the superstructure. That is all."

Bob looked at Gary. "Well?"

Gary looked about at the wet and dirty chaos. "This place is like a king-sized booby trap. So help me! We're safer on deck. Let's go, matie!"

They struggled into foul-weather gear and clawed their way up deck, then scuttled down deck to reach the door of the compartment. They opened it and were hit with a blast of cold wind, driving stinging salt spray against their heated faces. They clawed their way to the lifeline and worked their way aft. The sea was a frightening sight. The wind *had* increased and the surface of the sea was completely covered with long white patches of foam. Everywhere the edges of the wave crests were being blown into froth.

Gary looked back at Bob and shook his head. This was a storm now, perhaps winds of 55 to 66 miles per hour statute. If the wind kept increasing, it would reach Force 12, a hurricane.

Logie was no longer attempting to throw off the gray-beards that marched steadily out of the teeth of the wind and aboard the destroyer. She seemed to be welcoming them aboard. Now and then Bob looked back over his shoulder as the tin can pitched and slid down into a trough. Those waves must be thirty to forty feet in height, and it seemed to Bob that *Logie* was trying to punch a hole into the trough and keep on going down, down, and *down*. But each time she came up, bucking and shudder-

10

ing, creaking and groaning. The pumps were working steadily. Bob hoped they wouldn't have to work any harder. There was an awful lot of water out there, far more than *Logie* could drink in and still stay afloat.

They clung onto the lifeline as they saw Chief West, his weather gear dark with water and his broad brown face glistening with it. Some volunteers were floundering around on the fantail, one arm hooked over a lifeline and the other busy trying to secure the mess that had broken loose. Oil drums, planks, fenders, and lines were in a seemingly inextricable tangle, thundering about, lashing out at fragile human bodies like an insensate thing, to cripple or to kill.

The chief looked at Bob and Gary and jerked a thumb toward the motor whaler. The boat hung down by the after falls, its bows in the water one moment, only to lift the next moment and crash sickeningly against the destroyer's side. " We'll have a try at securing that," said the chief. " If we can't secure it, we'll cut it adrift. Don't take any chances. It isn't worth it. We don't want to start any more plates if we can help it, and that banging against the hull isn't helping us any. You lads game? "

Bob nodded. He and Gary had had plenty of practice in stormy weather, for both of them had served along the Aleutian Chain in the early part of the war, when the Japanese still held Kiska and Attu. They had been young civilians then, on board the good old *Otter,* ninety-eight feet of one of the best sea boats in the North Pacific.

Three more volunteers showed up, and Chief West, as though he was stalking a dangerous beast, which in a sense he was, directed his men. Time and time again the boat swung out only to smash back against the side of the destroyer. Time and time again the bow falls were almost

11

hooked on only to be torn from the grasp by the pulling of the boat or the wind. Solid water hit the plunging bows and cascaded thickly down the deck to wash knee-deep, and sometimes even waist-deep, about the struggling men. They were as soaked as though they didn't have on foul-weather gear.

Once *Logie* rolled, and *rolled*, until it seemed as though she would take solid water down her stacks, and for several terrifying moments Bob thought she was going right over. He hung on, waiting for that last sickening lurch, but *Logie* wasn't quite ready to say quits. She shuddered and strained, and then slowly, ever so slowly, she began to right herself.

" Almost on her beam ends," said Chief West. He shook his head. " A few more like that . . ." His voice trailed off into the howling wind.

It was getting almost impossible to distinguish sea from air. The waves rose to fearful heights, and as they did so their tops were ripped off by the wind to be blown away in great ribbons of foam which mingled with the horizontally driving rain that now swept down out of the murk ahead.

The men had given up trying to smother the rolling gear on the fantail. As *Logie* rolled, they pushed the tangle overboard yard by yard until at last a great sea tore it all away. Chief West waved the men into shelter, but a few of them stayed to help with the whaler. " Once more, dear hearts! " yelled Chief West.

Gary hung way out with a lifeline looped about his lean waist, extending a boathook to grip the lashing falls. He hooked the falls and began to draw them in toward clutching hands when *Logie* plunged deeply, corkscrewed, then lurched wildly from side to side. Something snapped. A

12

davit broke loose, dropping the bow of the whaler into the sea. The sea tore at it, driving it out and away from the salt-streaked side of the hull. Gary went with it, hanging on to the boathook.

"Let go, you fool!" screamed the chief.

It was too late. The force of the seas hurled the water-filled whaler farther outboard, dragging Gary with it. The after davit shuddered and something snapped sharply. The whaler swirled aft toward the submerged fantail with Gary hanging onto the parted falls. In a moment he had vanished into the darkness aft of the plunging destroyer.

"Gary!" yelled Bob into the howling madness of the storm.

A great graybeard silently climbed the down-plunging bows of *Logie* and raced aft, laced with foam, thick and solid and looking for a victim. It got one. Solid water struck Bob's legs, mounted to his waist and then his chest. His grip was torn loose and he went over the side, going down deep. The next upsurge flung him high, so that he was on a level with the rising fantail of the destroyer and he saw her screws racing as they left water. As he was carried down into the next trough he saw a seaman releasing a raft that tumbled into the gray, heaving waters. Then *Logie* was gone, as though erased by a giant and invisible hand.

He seemed safe enough from being submerged. His life jacket held his head high and the waves carried him along like a chip. Sure, he was safe enough from being submerged, but it was only a matter of time before the sea would win. It always did.

He was all alone and had never felt so alone in his entire lifetime. It was as though the whole solid world had vanished, leaving him in a limbo of water and air, to drift

13

on and on until he died of thirst, hunger, or exposure, or a combination of all three. He closed his eyes against the stinging spray and prayed.

High, high he rose and then slid down a long, foam-streaked slope. Something nudged his back and a fear of sharks lanced through his mind. Once again he was nudged. He turned his head and saw the rough bluish-gray surface of a life raft, festooned with lifeline. He reached out just as the sea moved the raft away from him, caught a line, pulled it closer, then caught it with his other hand. He pulled himself to the raft and with a last surge of strength got up over the side and dropped into it. He fell face downward and thanked God for his incredible fortune.

Bob sat up, clinging to the lifeline, and peered into the flying scud. Somewhere out there was Gary. If he was still afloat. The raft rose high and then plunged down into a trough. As it rose again, Bob saw something that seemed different, but it was lost beyond the next wave. Once again the raft lifted, poised, and plunged down again, and once again Bob saw something. His heart seemed to catch. It was the almost-submerged whaler, but there was no sign of Gary Lunt aboard it. He must have been torn away by the screaming wind or the powerful seas.

The raft rose again and plunged down, this time Bob saw the whaler on the side of the trough rather than on the crest of the next wave. The raft was drifting far faster than the whaler. Minutes dragged past and at last the raft and the whaler were on the same slope together. The raft charged down on the whaler and Bob saw something move within the boat. A head showed, staring incredulously at the raft. The raft surged toward the boat. They struck together and in that instant Bob reached inside the

whaler and gripped Gary by the high collar of his life
jacket. Somehow, in a fraction of a second, he had enough
strength to haul him halfway out of the boat. The wave
did the rest, tumbling Gary headfirst into the raft. The
whaler surged behind the raft and as it lifted on the next
wave it suddenly dropped out of sight to plunge to the
bottom fathoms below.

2

THE sea was empty except for the raft. As far as the eye could see, there was nothing but the heaving waters stirred by the strong breeze, the waves capped with fresh white foam like frosting on a cake, rising and falling, rising and falling while the raft dipped and bobbed in concert with them.

"You'd think they'da used a little imagination," grumbled Gary as he poked about in the can of rations that had been lashed in the raft. "A little relish wouldn't have taken up much room. These biscuits are like a chunk of wallboard."

Bob turned wearily. "Twenty-four hours ago you were up to your neck in cold seawater in a watery world, with minutes to go before that whaler sank under you. Now, you've got to gripe about the chow! Maybe they should have had a caterer come in. Maybe you want a chocolate soda instead of fresh water?"

Gary shook his head. "I'd settle for a thick malt," he said.

Bob rolled his eyes upward. "Give me strength," he muttered between clenched teeth.

"We've been in worse spots than this," said Gary.

"I can't recall any," said Bob.

"Think!" said Gary. He handed Bob a makeshift sand-

16

wich of hard sea biscuit and pork luncheon meat.

Bob settled with his back against the side of the raft. The storm had blown itself out or else they had passed beyond its wild domain. By now *Logie* must be hundreds of miles away. They wouldn't hang around looking for that plane or for the two men lost overboard in the storm. Who could have survived in that howling maelstrom?

Gary eyed the water breaker dubiously. " What's the odds, Mac? " he asked quietly. " There's not too much water in that breaker."

Bob did not look at him. "We're somewhere between the Carolines to the west and the Marshalls and Gilberts to the east."

" Jolly," said Gary. He bit into the sandwich. " You wouldn't happen to have a kosher dill pickle in your pocket, would you? "

" There's a lot of water out here," said Bob.

Gary nodded. He looked up at the clouded sky. " Do we control this area or do they? "

Bob shrugged. " A little bit of both. Like the old no-man's-land in World War I."

" I'd settle for a little bit of that land."

" I think we're drifting westerly," said Bob.

" To where? "

Bob munched his sandwich. "Who knows? The Admiralties are somewhere out there. Maybe New Guinea. It's a long way, kid."

Gary looked up at the sky and down at the sea. " Sure is, any way you look," he said.

Bob finished his sandwich. He was still hungry, but they would have to ration themselves, perhaps even more than they were doing now. It was the water that bothered him more than the food. A faint, far-off humming noise came to him. " What's that? " he asked.

Gary was justly famous for his excellent hearing. He looked up. " Plane," he said.

" Out here? "

" We were looking for one of our recon planes out here, weren't we? That wouldn't be the only one. If they have one, they'll have others."

" Ours or theirs? " Bob asked.

Gary looked quickly at him. " I never thought of that," he said quickly.

The humming sound came closer, then faded away, then came closer again, but there was nothing to be seen up there except the low-hanging strata of clouds.

" He's looking for something," said Gary softly, almost as though the flier could hear him. He looked at Bob. " Have they got any long-distance recon planes? "

" They've got a flying boat, nicknamed by us a *Mavis*, or something like that."

" Where would it come from? "

" Truk most likely. That's in the Carolines, somewhere northwest of where we are now."

" Great," murmured Gary.

" He's coming closer! " snapped Bob. " Get down! "

They lay flat in the bottom of the raft, keeping their faces down, thrusting their hands underneath themselves. One of the worst things one could do when a low-flying enemy plane appeared was to stare up at it, for the lightness of a face could be seen much farther than the rest of the clothed body.

Closer and closer came the plane until it was no longer a humming but a steady, though intermittent-sounding noise of more than one engine. Bob closed his eyes. There was one thing he did know: Japanese engines had that

18

intermittent sound as opposed to the steady roaring of American planes.

He tilted his head a little. Just below the layer of clouds he saw the wide-winged flying boat, moving leisurely along. There was no question now as to who it was.

"PBY?" whispered Gary hoarsely.

"No," Bob muttered.

They lay still, feeling the raft surge up and down beneath them, and soon the roaring of the motors began to die away. In a little while, there was only a faint humming to the north.

Gary sat up. "What about dessert?"

"You never give up, do you?"

"Nope," said Gary. He looked about. "Maybe we can rig a sail. We can take your shirt and pants, but we haven't got anthing for a mast."

"We've got you," said Bob dryly.

"Yo ho ho," chortled Gary. "We got a comedian in the boat."

Bob lay back against the side of the raft. He knew Gary was trying to keep up his spirits. It was just like him. But underneath, Gary knew as well as Bob did what their chances were. There was indeed a lot of water out there and it was an area not completely controlled by the Allied forces. He stared out to sea and was about to make a comment to Gary when he thought he saw something appear for a moment up out of the heaving waters and then disappear. "Gary," he said.

"Yes?"

"I — oh — nothing — I was only thinking."

"Hurts your little head, does it?"

Bob tried to keep any expression from his face but he could not take his eyes from the area where he had seen that mysterious something appear and disappear. He scanned the tumbling waters until his eyes began to ache. He turned to speak to Gary and as he did so he saw the same thing he had seen before and a queer feeling settled in the pit of his stomach. It looked like a heavy stick or branch floating upright in the water, like a spar buoy, but it didn't bob or sway like a stick or a spar buoy. It seemed steady in the water, as though it was attached to something under the water. Something big enough and heavy enough not to impart much motion to the stick, or whatever it was.

"The Japs got any subs around here?" Gary asked casually.

"Who knows?" said Bob carelessly, trying to keep the tension out of his voice.

"You *know* they do, Mac," said Gary.

There was no use in keeping the truth from Gary. Somewhere west of the raft, beneath the heaving surface of the sea, was a submarine, for it was the periscope Bob had seen, sliding up for a quick look-see, and vanishing again. He wasn't familiar enough with periscopes to be able to differentiate an American, British, or Japanese periscope one from the other, although he had had several harrowing and dangerous experiences with Japanese I-Boats in the Aleutians, and the memories were still painfully fresh.

"Gary," said Bob softly, "don't look now, but there's a sub prowling around, watching us through the periscope."

"Yeh," said Gary. "I know. Funny, isn't it? I was hesitating to tell *you* about it like you was *me*."

Bob couldn't help cringing. "The English! Hooeee!"

"Ya unnerstan me, don'tcha! That's all you have to know!"

20

The periscope slid up again and took a longer look. It was no more than two hundred yards from them.

"What a shot," said Gary.

"You couldn't hit that broomstick from here with a 20mm.," said Bob.

"I'd like to try, just the same."

The periscope vanished. Minutes ticked past. Bob felt the pit of his stomach form into a ball of ice. Somewhere underneath those peaceful-looking waters was a long cigar of steel, packed like a huge clock with machinery, torpedoes, and equipment — probably the most concentrated and deadly machine of war that mind of man had ever invented and developed. It was taking its good-natured time to scout the raft and the two helpless American seamen aboard it.

"Maybe they left," said Gary hoarsely.

Even as he spoke, there was a roaring of water behind them. They turned to see a sharklike prow rearing itself out of the sea with foaming water cascading from it. A long, black-painted hull, scabrous with rust patches and leprous white streaks rose from the depths. The conning tower appeared, forcing a passage though the water. The submarine began to level off with water flowing from the rounded deck and streaming from the many freeing ports along the lean hull.

Bob closed his eyes. "Thank God," he managed to say. The sub was American, all right — a fleet-type submarine of the latest kind.

"Maybe she was captured and is manned by Nips," said Gary. "That'd be just our luck."

"You've got a lovely sense of humor," said Bob.

Hatch covers flipped open on the submarine, and men appeared on the dripping bridge. Commands were spat

21

out, but they were unintelligible to the boys on the pitching raft. The submarine moved closer, heaving and rolling easily, with water flowing freely across the upper decking.

A seaman appeared on the foredeck with a line in his hands. As the sub neared the raft, he threw it skillfully toward the raft. Gary caught it neatly and made it fast. Several other sailors helped pull the raft toward the submarine.

"Make it snappy!" roared a hard voice from the bridge. "I don't enjoy sitting here like a ruptured duck with Jap patrol planes up in that overcast. *Let's gooooooo!*"

Bob clambered clumsily up the side of the submarine, followed by Gary. "What about the raft?" said Bob.

"You goin' to miss it that much?" said the grinning sailor who had heaved the line to them. "Move! The skipper is giving us about two minutes to get below or we'll all need that raft to get back to Pearl!"

They raced toward the conning tower across the wet wooden slats of the decking. The submariner led the way into the steel "sail," which enclosed cigarette deck, periscope shears, and bridge deck.

"Get below!" came the acrid voice from the bridge. "Lookouts! Stand by to dive!"

Bob tumbled down the ladder into the control room, crowded to capacity with dials, lights, men, and gear of all kinds. Gary was right behind him. They were rushed through an open watertight door into the forward battery room.

"Last man, sir!" snapped the voice of a lookout from the control room.

"Clear the bridge!"

"Clear the bridge! Dive! Dive! Dive!" The sharp commands were instantly followed by three raucous blasts of a klaxon horn. A hatch banged shut. The boat tilted forward and down. Water was heard rushing swiftly through the freeway beneath the deck superstructure.

"Welcome aboard, fellows," said a greasy-looking character to Bob and Gary.

"Glad to be aboard," said Bob.

"You have no idea," murmured Gary. "When do we submerge?"

The motormac grinned. "You're under *now*, Mac."

"You guys don't fool around, do you?" said Gary.

"Name is Slim Polk."

"Bob Dunbar," said Bob.

"Gary Lunt," said Gary. "What ship is this?"

"Ship?" said Slim. "This is a *boat*. You always call a sub a boat. We're the *Grayfin*," he added proudly.

"She's nearly as big as a destroyer," said Gary.

"She's still a *boat*, Mac. Get forward into the wardroom. The skipper wants to talk to you."

They walked slightly downhill as the submarine kept sliding down into the depths. On either side of them were tiny staterooms sealed off by swinging green curtains. Above them came the purring of a hidden motor, doing one of the many functions required to keep this fighting machine functioning efficiently. There was an acid smell from the massive batteries beneath the deck. They stepped into the wardroom on their left. Leather-upholstered benches and a table covered with dark-green cloth dominated the little room. On every available surface were pictures of enemy planes and ships. Stenciled on the surface of a locker were a number of Rising Sun emblems, indicative of planes and ships sunk by *Grayfin*. Gary whistled softly. He pointed at the emblems. "This *boat* has been around," he whispered.

A tall, broad-shouldered officer wearing commander's insignia came in and looked at them. "Welcome aboard," he said.

"Glad to be aboard, sir," they choroused.

"I'm Commander Gil Currie, skipper of *Grayfin*."

"Robert Dunbar, Signalman Second Class, sir," said Bob.

"Gary Lunt, Gunner's Mate Third Class, sir," said Gary.

"Sit down," said the officer. He took off his hat. "Kelly! Bring three cups of joe!"

"Yes, sir!" came a muffled voice from the pantry forward of the wardroom.

"How did you lads happen to be out rafting?" asked Commander Currie.

"We were aboard the *Logie*, sir," said Bob. "A destroyer. We were on our way to Brisbane from Kwajalein and ran into that storm a day or so ago. We had been damaged by shore batteries and had been ordered to Brisbane for a refit. On the way we were diverted to look for a downed and lost reconnaissance plane, but the storm caught up with us. We had all we could do to stay afloat. Lunt and I were helping to make fast a motor whaler that was breaking loose. Both of us got washed overboard. Someone dropped us a raft. We were lucky enough to find it, sir."

The redheaded messman served the coffee. "You got more luck than you deserve," he said. "How about that, sir?"

Currie nodded. "An angel was watching over you. We could use some of that luck, if it *is* luck."

Gary sipped the coffee. "*Grayfin* is heading for the barn, I hope," he said.

"No," said the officer.

24

Bob looked up. " Can you send a message about us being picked up, sir? " he asked.

" No," said the officer.

" May I ask where we are going, sir? " asked Bob.

Currie emptied his cup. " No," he said for the third time.

Bob flushed. " Maybe I said something wrong."

Currie shook his head. " No." He smiled. " I can't tell you anything now. You need chow, a bunk, and some sleep. Kelly, take them aft and take care of them."

Kelly led the way back through the forward battery room, the control room, the galley, and into the crew's mess. While they waited, he rustled up a pair of blankets. The boys were served from the galley. The cook grinned at them. " This is the deluxe treatment for pickups," he said. " The one and only time."

Gary stared at the food. " This is officers' chow, isn't it? " he said incredulously.

" Better," said the cook.

Gary rolled his eyes upward. " And here I've been serving on a tin can all this time," he said.

Kelly sat down and studied Gary. " You don't look like an eatin' man," he said.

" Watch him," said Bob dryly.

Kelly sipped at his coffee. " The officers eat the same chow we do. It's all cooked in the same galley."

" Noble of them," said Gary around a mouthful of food.

" We're still working on the fresh food," said the cook through the window from the galley. " Then we go on to the frozen stuff. If we're out long enough, you start in on the canned stuff. That's a dandy combination, I tell you. A tired crew that's been out too long and canned food. It should be the other way around. Fresh food for a tired crew, not for a fresh crew."

Kelly emptied his cup. " Have you ever tried to figure out how that could be done, Blascovitz? " he asked.

The cook shook his head. " I've been working on it," he said.

" Maybe you could buy fresh chow from a Jap ship," said Gary.

Kelly wrinkled his nose. " Octopus steak. Raw fish. Rice. Sukiyaki, whatever *that* is."

" You want ice cream or mince pie for dessert, boys? " asked Blascovitz.

" Listen to him," said Gary. He smiled. " I'll have peach ice cream. Make it a la mode, Mac."

The cook shook his head. " No peach. Banana. Strawberry. Vanilla and chocolate."

Gary closed his eyes rapturously. " Could I have a scoop of each? " he asked wistfully.

" Sure thing! Like I said: This is the one and only time," answered the cook.

" Submarines," said Gary. " Man, I can hardly wait to transfer once we get back."

" If we *do* get back," said Kelly. " This isn't a patrol duty off the West Coast."

Blascovitz served the pie a la mode and sat down. " We've got advantages. We rate 'em. There are no Purple Hearts in the submarine service. You either come out whole or you don't come out at all."

Gary shoveled a load of pie and ice cream into his mouth and spoke around it. " Just where are we going? "

" Sealed orders," said the cook.

" You must have some idea," said Bob.

Kelly stood up. " Got to take care of my pantry," he said. " It's almost time for chow." He left the messroom.

"Talkative, isn't he?" murmured Gary.

Blascovitz began to clear the table. "He wouldn't know," he said.

"What do you think?" Gary questioned.

The cook shrugged. He carried the tray to the window and set it down. He looked back over his shoulder. "Japan," he said softly.

Gary's fork stopped halfway to his gaping mouth. A big dripping gob of pie and ice cream fell heavily to his plate. Bob looked at Gary. The same old icy feeling came to settle in the pit of his stomach beside the good food he had just taken aboard.

The cook came back to the table. "I don't know for sure," he said in a low, confidential voice, "but we got extra chow, ammo, and extra *everything*. This is my fifth patrol and I never seen anything like this."

"Maybe we're heading for Pearl," Gary said with a reassuring smile.

"Not on your life!" said the cook. "Why would we haul all that extra gear back to Pearl? No, it's Japan. Maybe the old Bungo Suido itself!"

"Bungo Suido?" said Bob curiously.

Blascovitz bobbed his head. "The ol' Inland Sea area. Bungo Suido is the strait between Shikoku and Kyushu Islands. Lots of shipping in there."

A young fellow, about the same age as Bob and Gary, came into the messroom. The name Fuller was stenciled on his shirt pocket. "I'm Dusty Fuller," he said with a pleasing smile. "Yeoman striker."

"Striker," said Blascovitz haughtily. "Lowest of all things."

The boy grinned. "I won't type any more letters home for you, Blas. I mean it this time." He looked at Bob and

Gary. "Chief Daly sent me to take you forward to your bunks. You'll have to hot-bunk it."

"Meaning?" asked Gary as he cleaned up his plate.

"You share a bunk with someone else."

"At the same time?"

Dusty grinned again. "No, only when he's on watch. We get a little crowded on this boat. You fellows ready?"

"Thanks," said Bob to Blascovitz.

"Think nothing of it," said the good-natured cook.

The yeoman striker led Bob and Gary forward through the narrow passageway, stepping high over the sills of the oval-shaped doors until they reached the forward torpedo room that converged toward the bows. At the forward end of the compartment were the rows of bright brass doors that closed the bow torpedo tubes, six in all. Torpedoes, coated with a thin brown preservative, were lashed on racks by the port and starboard bulkheads, above, below, and beside the sliding leather bunks. The after end of the compartment was fitted with a washbasin on the portside and a compartment about the size of a telephone booth containing a shower and a head on the starboard side.

"This is the coolest place for sleeping," said Dusty. "Farthest away from the engines."

"And closest to the enemy," said Gary.

Dusty shrugged. "What difference does that make? In a sub *everything* is close to everything else." He jerked a thumb toward a bunk. "That's yours, Gary."

Gary scrambled into it. "Hey," he said, "there's a torpedo right beside me."

"That's your bunkie," said Dusty. His face broke into another pleasing grin.

"This thing dangerous?" Gary asked uneasily.

28

"Only when you're on the receiving end of it," said Dusty.

Bob climbed into his bunk, missing one valve with his nose, cracking an elbow on another, bumping a knee on yet another. "Comfy," he said dryly.

"We're going to surface tonight to charge batteries," said Dusty. "You can get some fresh air then. I'll take you up. I'm on lookout. Sweet dreams, fellows." He left them to their own thoughts.

The boat was never quiet. There were hummings, throbbings, whirrings, whinings, and rushing sounds, with the constant vibration of the engines carrying through the hull. It was all blended together and it never stopped.

"Bob?"

"Yes?"

"Do you think the chow is worth it?"

Bob closed his eyes. He was dead beat and the bunk felt good. "All I know is that it's better than that raft."

There was a long silence. "Bob?"

"Yes?"

"What did he mean by that crack about there being no Purple Hearts in the submarine service? About coming out whole or not coming out at all?"

"Figure it out, Mac," said Bob quietly.

There was another long silence. "I did," Gary said. "I think he *meant* it too!"

Grayfin slid easily on through the dark depths of the sea, burrowing her way steadily onward, heading for someplace that even Commander Currie did not know and wouldn't know until he reached a certain latitude and longitude and was able to open his sealed orders. Until that time every officer and man aboard could only wonder and do a little cold sweating.

29

3

Rise and shine," said the cheerful voice in Bob's ear. "We're going to surface."

Bob opened his eyes to look up into the dim face of Dusty Fuller. He slammed himself back, feeling a valve bore into a shoulder. A strange-looking face it was indeed, with red-lensed goggles hiding the friendly blue eyes of the yeoman striker. "What's this? Halloween?" gasped Bob.

The boy shook his head. "I'm going on watch as lookout. We wear these goggles fifteen minutes before going on watch so as to get used to the difference in light between down here and on the surface. Get your shoes on. I got permission from the exec for you to come topside for a while. How do you feel?"

"Headache," said Bob.

Dusty nodded. "Figures. You'll get used to this air before we get back from this patrol."

"Never," said Bob.

Dusty grinned, looking like some kind of weird monster from Mars. "Wait until we get forced below from a depth charge attack or something. Man, the old air gets blue and you can draw pictures in it with a finger."

"I can hardly wait," said Bob.

Dusty reached across and tapped Gary. "Rise and shine,

30

Mac," he said in a low voice.

Gary rolled over, took one look at Dusty, and yelped in sudden fright. He slammed back into his bunk and wrapped his arms around the torpedo beside him. "Go away! I'll wake up and you won't be there!"

"Stow that gab!" yelled a man from another bunk.

Dusty placed a finger to his lips. He motioned Bob and Gary to follow him. The submarine deck was slanted upward as *Grayfin* started to surface. Commands sounded through the boat. Motors whirred and the various other sounds of the complicated machinery needed to control the fleet submarine sounded in unison, turned on and off, raised or lowered the sound. The interior of the submarine was filled with eerie, reddish light. Dusty led the way through the control room hatch. The place was filled with the round faces of many gauges and a mass of green and red lights in neat rectangular rows. "That's the Christmas Tree," whispered Dusty to Bob. "Shows the state of all the sub's valves and hull openings."

The men and officers in the control room did not look at the three intruders, although there was just about room enough for all of them, including other seamen standing by to go on lookout duty.

The surfacing alarm sounded. The boat was rising quickly. "Lookouts! Stand by to surface!" came the command.

The quartermaster opened the hatch and a shower of water came down. Air roared out through the opening. Instantly there was frenzied action as lookouts, officers, and others scrambled up into the fresh air, followed by two confused destroyermen. Water dripped everywhere and some of it poured down Bob's neck, thoroughly chilling him, but it was worth it to smell that blessed fresh air.

31

Dusty took his station on the cigarette deck aft of the periscope sheers and the radar antenna. He uncased his leather-covered night glasses and focused them on the propeller guards. He plugged in a rubberized telephone line and hung the phone about his neck. There were other lookouts on the platforms port and starboard of the periscope shears, and one forward.

Gary breathed in deeply. "I wish we'd stay up here from now on in."

"No chance," said Dusty over his shoulder. He was scanning the darkness out from the port quarter.

A young officer came aft from the bridge. "I'm Ensign Tolliver," he said pleasantly. "We'd rather you didn't talk to the lookout, men."

Gary glanced at Bob. On the *Logie* both of them would have been chewed out but good for talking to a lookout. There seemed to be an easy relationship between officers and men on a submarine, but perhaps the discipline was even tougher than on a tin can.

"How do you feel?" he asked Bob.

"Headachy, sir."

"You'll get over it. We'll be running on the surface for some hours to recharge the batteries and the air flasks."

The submarine was sliding along through the dark seas, with bluish smoke rising from the diesel exhausts. The diesels were pumping new life into her gigantic batteries. A seaman came up on deck. "Permission to dump garbage, sir?" he asked the bridge.

"Permission granted," came the acrid voice Bob remembered from when they were picked up. It was the voice of Lieutenant Mack Davis, the executive officer.

The weighted garbage was heaved over the side. Gary scratched his head. "How come?" he said.

"They don't want to leave any traces floating on the surface," said Bob.

"Crazeee!"

Bob shook his head. "These are as much Jap waters as they are ours," he said.

Dusty nodded but he did not speak. His glasses swung steadily back and forth as he peered out into the darkness.

Fresh air was being pumped into the boat into the high and low pressure lines and tanks. The water foamed back from the shark prow with a gentle *snick-snick-snick* to spread out in a wide whitish wake. *Grayfin* seemed to be moving in a world of her own, but she was not dreaming. In addition to the eyes of the lookouts, the radar was in operation and so was the sonar, the first probing the surface and the second probing the depths. The radarman and the sonarman were the real lookouts because the deck lookouts had little efficiency at night but every precaution must be taken. As deadly as a submarine was to the enemy, she was also in great danger from them. She had no armor. Her greatest defense was the depths of the sea and her maneuverability below the surface. A fleet submarine is more on the surface than she is below it, and is more of a submersible surface craft than a true submarine. Her time below the surface was limited.

A head popped up beside Bob and the broad, good-natured face of Blascovitz the cook appeared. "Have some Jolly Jacks," he said. He handed the boys a couple of candy bars apiece and began to peel one himself.

"Oh no!" said Gary.

"What's wrong, kid?" the cook wanted to know.

Gary looked at the candy bars. "Chocolate Carmel Delights," he said ruefully.

Bob grinned and then began to laugh.

"Let's keep it quieter out here," growled someone.

Blascovitz turned. "This is Chief of the Boat Daly," he said. "Owns a plank of the *Grayfin*. Been with her since she was launched at Mare Island. Have a Jolly Jack, Chief."

"I hate those blasted sticky things," said Daly. He looked at Bob and Gary. "Tin can men, eh? Well, I guess we've got to put up with you."

"Thanks, Chief," murmured Gary.

A pair of hard gray eyes bored into Gary's face. "You and your pal here just out of boot camp?"

"No, Chief," said Bob quickly. Gary had a knack of getting into trouble the instant he was in a new situation. This was one time Bob meant to keep his pal's record clean, if possible.

"What are your records?" asked the Chief.

"Both of us saw sea duty in the Aleutians as crewmen on a government-chartered transport boat," said Bob.

"Merchant Marine," said the chief with a note of disgust in his voice.

"Oh, I don't know," said Gary. "They've been holding up their end of the war. Murmansk Run and all that sort of stuff."

Once again the hard eyes stabbed at Gary. Gary would never learn. *Never!*

Bob couldn't tell the chief that they had participated in sinking a big Japanese I-Boat off Amchitka Island while the Japs still occupied Kiska and Attu. "We were on destroyer duty in the Slot," said Bob.

"What can?" said Daly.

"*MacRonan*," said Bob.

There was a faint, a *very* faint look of respect on the chief's face. "That isn't the one you got lost off," he said.

34

Bob shook his head. " *MacRonan* was mined in the Slot. Later, after some other duty, we were assigned aboard *Logie*."

The faint look of respect came back. Daly nodded. "What was that other duty?"

"PT's," said Gary laconically.

"A cake of soap in the bathtub," said the chief.

Gary inspected his chocolate-smeared fingertips. "Oh, I don't know," he said.

Bob moved in again. "We were only on temporary duty with a PT boat," he said. "It was lost."

Daly raised an eyebrow. "How did you get off of it?"

"We weren't on it at the time," said Gary.

Daly leaned against the rail. "Now, bright boy," he said to Gary. "Tell me *where* you were."

Gary smiled. "On an island."

"Like Robinson Crusoe?" murmured the chief.

"Not exactly," said Gary. "We got pretty busy after a while, making like Ferdinand the Bull. Coast-watching, you know."

"You *do* get around," said the chief softly.

Bob wet his dry lips. Gary was already maneuvering to get into trouble. He had been in trouble with Chief West on *MacRonan*, and later he had tangled with Lieutenant Bennick, an administrative officer on Foofoofarongo, the Devil's Island for seamen without a ship. By a miracle Bob and Gary had managed to escape from the enraged Bennick by being temporarily assigned aboard a PT boat that by good fortune had arrived at Foofoofarongo short two crewmen. The very night the PT had sailed for her base, Gary had managed to dump a full box of melting Chocolate Caramel Delights over Ensign Kovac, the tough-as-nails exec of the PT boat. It wouldn't have been so bad

35

except that some weeks later Gary had casually mentioned to a new crew member that Ensign Kovac just loved half-melted Chocolate Caramel Delights. That event had almost led to the first murder of a seaman by an officer of the United States Navy in World War II.

Bob smiled wanly at the chief. " Well, we were picked up by an Aussie coast watcher. Things got pretty rough, so we worked with him until we could get off the island."

" We took over from him," said Gary loftily.

" I'll bet," said Daly.

" No kidding," said Gary.

Bob looked about for a place of escape, but there *was* no escape. After Bob and Gary had returned to sea duty, sporting a brand-new Silver Star apiece for their work as substitute coast watchers, they had been reassigned under their old commanding officer of the *MacRonan*, Commander Roberts, aboard the brand-new *Logie*. Gary and Bob had been heroes for one week and then, with the inevitable plot of a Greek tragedy, Gary had run afoul of Chief West, who was also serving on *Logie*, as he had on *MacRonan*. There was no end to the tangled skeins Gary Lunt could weave with a disarming nonchalance that was positively deadly.

" Maybe you made a hero out of yourself," said Daly to Gary.

" Maybe we better get below," said Bob hollowly.

" No," said the chief. " Wait! I want to hear this."

Gary finished his candy bar and wiped his chocolaty hands. " Got a Silver Star," said Gary airily. " Want to shake hands with a hero, Chief? "

" I don't deserve the honor," said Daly dryly. He looked at Bob. " Did you get a Silver Star too? "

" He should'a got the Navy Cross," said Gary. " Lotsa

old-timers in this man's Navy get 'em for twenty years' service, or so I hear."

" As easy as that, eh? " said the chief.

Gary nodded. " They issue them out when the old-timers creak up to reenlist."

Daly's face was set hard and his eyes were fixed like a basilisk on the smiling face of Gary Lunt, Gunner's Mate Third Class, and Fool's Mate First Class.

Bob cleared his throat. " Can we do anything aboard this ship, Chief? I don't want to sit around in the way for this patrol. I've done plenty of lookout duty."

" Boat! " snapped Daly. " Not ship! Get *that* straight anyway! "

" We can use a couple of extra hands," said Ensign Tolliver from the shadows. He had evidently sensed the friction between Chief Daly and Gary.

" I'll see to it," Daly said. He turned on a heel and stamped off.

Tolliver shoved back his hat. He looked at Gary. " You do a fine job of riling up a man," he said quietly.

" I was only kidding, sir," said Gary, with a red face.

" Do you and Dunbar really have Silver Stars? "

" Yes, sir," said Gary proudly.

" Congratulations," said Tolliver. " It so happens that Chief Daly has a Medal of Honor from World War I and a Navy Cross from this one, and he didn't creak up to re-enlist to get either of them."

" Oh," said Gary.

" The best thing for you to do, young man," Tolliver said, " is to keep your mouth shut until you learn the score. It so happens that a submarine crew is handpicked. Each man must be physically perfect, even if he is as old as Chief Daly. Each candidate for submarine service is care-

37

fully and exhaustively tested for any psychological quirks that might endanger the boat and the crew. One minor mistake in judgment, one wrong turning of a valve, one hesitation — anything like that and the boat and crew could be lost. We spend weeks at sea, hours and hours *under* the sea, fighting Japs, bad air, boredom, and fatigue and we can't afford to have men aboard who can't stand up to it. This is a good boat and a good crew. They work well and fight well together, and there is a personal loyalty here that is hard to define. Remember that, as long as you are aboard."

"Hear, hear," said a hard voice.

Bob looked around to see the face of Lieutenant Davis, the executive officer. "What's the matter with Daly?" the officer asked Ensign Tolliver.

Tolliver shrugged. "He's feeling a little low, I suppose."

Davis eyed the two castaways. "That so? Unusual for him. He tells me you two men want some sort of duty."

"Anything, sir!" said Bob.

"We can use a galley hand. How about you?"

"I'm a signalman, sir. I've done lookout on destroyers and a PT boat."

The exec nodded. "I'll have him post you as lookout. Any radar or sonar experience?"

"A little, sir."

"We can use you as striker, if you like."

"I'd like that, sir."

The green eyes swiveled and fixed themselves on Gary. "Any objections to working in the galley?"

Gary kept a straight face. Oh, joy! Working in a sub galley was about as close to heaven as Gary could get on this old earth. "No, sir," he said.

"All right. Report to Stan Blascovitz. You can double as lookout."

"Yes, sir," said Gary.

Davis started to walk forward. He turned. "You can always apologize to the chief of the boat," he said. "He doesn't hold grudges." Then he was gone.

"How did he know what happened?" said Bob.

"The chief must'a told him," said Gary bitterly.

Tolliver shook his head. "You know better than that. An exec knows all and sees all, and Mack Davis is the best exec I have ever served with, bar none." He looked up at the dark sky. "Now get below and let some of the others come up for air. From here on we'll be spending a lot of time with a lot of water on top of us and even when we're on the surface, there won't be much time for any of us to shoot the breeze on the cigarette deck."

Bob led the way below into the conning tower, the hatch outlined with faint bluish light. The conning tower was a miniature of the control room below it. The red-lighted control room was filled with men who ignored the two castaways, their eyes fixed on their particular duty. The helmsman stood with his hands on the wheel, making slow adjustments to the designated course. The sonar watch was swinging the underwater sound receiver. The radarman was scanning his screen, watching the "grass" flickering on it, waiting for a pip to show. A freckle-faced officer was bent over a navigating chart.

"Let's put a strain on the coffee urn," whispered Gary as they walked aft to the galley.

The galley had quite a few crewmen in it. Some of them looked curiously at the two newcomers. A game of acey-deucey was in full swing. A towheaded torpedoman was laboriously writing a letter. A bald-headed motormac was

39

reading a worn-looking magazine. Music was coming softly from a speaker on the bulkhead. It was the " Stars and Stripes Forever " being played by a fine military band.

Gary kept time with his spoon as he sipped at his coffee.

The march music stopped. " Good evening, you American boys out there," came a cultured contralto voice. " This is Tokyo Rose speaking. Did you like the nice music? Did it make you homesick? You really should be home with your loved ones. Your wives, mothers, and sweethearts are pining for you, American boys at sea and in the jungles. It is so sad that you must all die while your leaders are safe at home and the civilians are making all the money and dating your girls. We know where every soldier's outfit is and where every ship and submarine is located. We Japanese do not want to kill you, but because you are the invaders we will have to do it.

" Would you like some news from home? The longshoremen are striking for higher wages. How much are *you* being paid? A dollar a day? Too bad so many of you are dying each day for that kind of money.

" And now for news of particular units and ships of the United States Army and Navy. The destroyer U.S.S. *Logie* has been reported as lost at sea in a typhoon."

Gary dropped his spoon. Bob's head snapped up.

" Your ship? " said an electrician's mate to Bob.

Bob nodded dumbly.

" Tough luck," said the bald-headed motormac.

" The U.S.S. submarine *Grayfin* left Brisbane about a week ago for patrol duty in the Central Pacific. Poor old *Grayfin!* Why don't they let you go back to the barn at Pearl for a rest? Isn't this at least your tenth war patrol? Let some of the others take over for a while. The longer you stay out here, fellows, the better the chances for our brave and efficient Antisubmarine Service to get you. And they will, *Grayfin*. They will . . ." Her smooth unaccented voice trailed off to be followed by symphonic music.

The letter writer looked up. " How did she know we were out here on patrol? " he asked quietly.

The bald-headed man looked up from his magazine. " Don't let it bother you, Barney. Listen to the music. At least that's true."

Barney shook his head. " How does she know, Baldy? My cousin was on *Corvina* on her first patrol off Truk last November. On the thirtieth or thereabouts she was sent dispatches two nights in a row. She never acknowledged them. She was given up for lost December twenty-third."

" What's that got to do with Tokyo Rose? " asked an acey-deucey player.

Barney leaned forward. " On the eighteenth of November, Tokyo Rose announced that *Corvina* was off Truk. Two days later she said a Jap I-Boat had torpedoed *Corvina*."

" Go on," said Gary.

" How did *she* know *Corvina* was off Truk? " said Barney.

It was very quiet in the messroom. " Maybe she knew when *Corvina* was sunk," said Chief Daly from the doorway. He walked to the coffee urn and began to fill a cup. " She kept the information to herself a few days, announcing that she had advance information on *Corvina*, then announced she had been sunk, after she *knew* it was *Corvina*."

" How about that! " said Gary.

The chief sat down and looked about. " I've been on eight war patrols in this boat and two or three times she named *Grayfin*. We got back every time and we're going

41

to get back this time." His quiet voice seemed to reassure everyone.

Gary looked down at the chief. "I want to apologize, Chief," he said.

Every eye was on Gary. The chief looked away. "You don't have to do it in front of everyone, Lunt," he said gruffly.

Gary shook his head. "I want to do it that way, Chief. I've got a big mouth."

"Who doesn't, kid?" said the chief. "Now forget it!"

Later, as Bob was in his bunk, listening to the myriad noises of a submarine at sea, running on the surface to recharge batteries, the voice of Tokyo Rose came back to him. "*The longer you stay out there, fellows, the better the chances for our brave and efficient Antisubmarine Service to get you. And they will, Grayfin. They will. . . .*"

4

GRAYFIN was submerged and running easily with a week logged up, and no one, not even Commander Currie, knew what her ultimate destination would be. Day after day she ran submerged, and at dusk she came to the surface to make better time and to recharge her batteries and air flasks. The patrol seemed routine, and new men and veterans had settled down to the rhythm of it, but there was an air of tension in the boat. Two nights running Tokyo Rose had mentioned *Grayfin*, and although no one had spoken about it, it was certainly in everyone's mind. She had also mentioned the recent loss of *Sculpin*, missing since sometime in November.

Gary seemed happy enough. Under the expert guidance of Cook First Class Stanley Blascovitz, he was making inroads into the lore of seagoing cooking as well as inroads into the great store of food that seemed to fill every available extra space in the submarine. Gary had happily tallied off some of the stores to Bob one evening over a game of chess. "Seventy gallons of Coke syrup! Six hundred pounds of coffee! Enough candy to fill every Christmas stocking in a good-sized town! Cartridge bottles to charge water for mixing the Coke syrup! The old 'chill box' is full of meat and ice cream! The reefer is jam full! The food storerooms are full! Old Blascovitz gets me to go around making like an inventory of nonperishables tucked here and there throughout this boat. Man, this stuff is wedged into corners, over pipes, under this and under that."

Bob had listened to the delirious chatter, but a memory came back to settle uneasily in his mind. "We're still working on the fresh food," Stan Blascovitz had said the first night the boys had been on board. "Then we go into the frozen stuff. If we're out long enough, we start in on the canned stuff. That's a dandy combination, I tell you. A tired crew that's been out too long and canned food."

At the end of the first week the fresh food was almost depleted and still *Grayfin* forged on.

Bob enjoyed his temporary duties. He liked lookout because it gave him plenty of time on deck during the hours of darkness as *Grayfin* surfaced to recharge her batteries. While she was submerged, Bob worked as sonarman striker under calm and efficient Sonarman First Class Eddie Scarlotti. It was a fascinating duty. Bob had had a little experience with it aboard *Logie,* but not enough to satisfy him. He had plenty of time for it now. A good part of the *Grayfin* crew switched around from one duty to another when times were right for it. Commander Currie was a firm believer in the theory that each man in his crew should know as much about other duties as he could in case of emergency, and emergencies were quite common in the Silent Service.

Grayfin broke the surface one evening for her usual surface run that would keep on until the gray light of the false dawn if radar, sonar, and lookouts didn't spot anything suspicious. Everyone and everything seemed to be an enemy to a submarine. Even friendly surface, undersea, and air craft took no chances. More than one friendly sub-

44

marine had been torpedoed, or bombed, or shelled by its own friends.

Bob scuttled up the ladder slightly damp with the water that had poured in when the hatch had been opened. In a matter of minutes the bridge watch, lookouts, and officers were topside, even as the seas were still parting aside from the lean hull of the submersible.

The air was fresh and damp, although slightly warm. The sharp bow of the submarine cut through the calm seas, spreading a wide wash of foam freckled with phosphorescence. Bob tied the leather sling of the night glasses to the rail of the cigarette deck, then raised them to focus on the starboard propeller guard. He plugged in the phone and looked about. The sea was calm, with a slight ripple. There were clouds, but a faint tinge of moonlight was in the sky. It might be nearly as bright as day that night and lookouts would have to be especially alert. The white wake of the submarine would be clearly visible to night-flying Japanese planes. In addition, the Japanese Navy was second to none in the matter of trained visual lookouts and their night glasses were far superior to those of the United States Navy. Even with radar and sonar, as well as lookouts, some U.S. Navy units had been surprised by the Japanese at Savo Island, suffering one of the worst defeats the United States Navy had ever experienced. They had been completely surprised, and the efficiency of Japanese lookouts and their excellent night glasses had, in a large part, been responsible for the Japanese surprise.

The submarine rolled ever so slightly in the soft swells, parting them easily. Bob went through the rhythm of a lookout, swinging his glasses from a point centered on the starboard beam aft to the narrow stern, thence back up the other side. His area was partly covered as well by the two lookouts, port and starboard.

Bob seemed self-hypnotized as he worked. Once he thought he saw something far to starboard, but after studying it, he shook his head. He was beginning to see " bogeys " that didn't exist. It was getting lighter now, but Commander Currie would keep on the surface as long as he could. The diesels were roaring steadily at all ahead, standard as *Grayfin* forged on through enemy waters.

" Bridge! " rasped the speaker. " Contact on radar bearing three-three-oh, range fifty thousand yards! "

" Control," said Lieutenant Davis, " keep radar ranges coming."

Bob swung his glasses to cover the area. It was the same area where he *thought* he had seen a bogey.

Minutes ticked past as *Grayfin* plunged on.

" Bridge! " said the speaker. " I have three sure pips on the radar now, sir. Might be a convoy."

" Or a trio of destroyers or cruisers," said the officer. " Keep them coming, Bader."

Was Davis planning to close with the three unknown vessels? Supposing they were destroyers or cruisers? No sub commander in his right mind would tangle with such a deadly trio. The *Grayfin* might get one, but she'd never get the other two, and more than likely they'd get her. They had the odds. Bob scanned the area where the vessels had been located by radar, although he knew very well he wouldn't see anything.

" Bridge! " said the speaker. " Radar bearing three-three-oh, range forty-five thousand yards."

The engine room annunciators tinkled faintly and in a few moments all four Fairbanks-Morse diesel engines were pounding away roaring steadily with exhaust smoke rising from the stern of the speeding submarine. Mack Davis was eager to close with the strange ships.

Minutes swept past the bullnose of the *Grayfin* as she raced on toward the three unseen ships.

"Bridge!" said the speaker. "Radar bearing three-three-two, range thirty-eight thousand yards."

"We're gaining," said Red Kelly, the port lookout.

"On what?" asked Bob. "A bunch of mean-looking Jap tin cans?"

"That's what we're here for, Mac," said Kelly.

"Quiet!" roared Mack Davis.

Bob was sure the Japs could have heard that bull-roaring voice of the exec. He raised his glasses and searched the area where the ships were located, but as before, he was unable to see anything.

Time crept past. The moonlight began to lighten the heaving surface of the sea and the black hull of the speeding submarine began to stand out as the waters turned silvery. If the Japs couldn't hear the roaring of those engine exhausts, they could surely spot the black hull and conning tower of *Grayfin*.

"Radar bearing three-three-three, range thirty thousand yards," screeched the bridge speaker.

"Wake up the skipper," said Mack Davis. "He'll want to take over."

Bob felt the cold sweat break out on him. Surely they weren't going to close with those Japanese warships on the surface. That was madness. Yet, they'd never be able to close with the enemy while submerged. Bob began to appreciate the niceties of timing in submarine warfare. It was a little too finely cut to suit Mrs. Dunbar's favorite son Robert.

The next ranging was twenty-eight thousand yards, and just then Commander Currie came up onto the little

47

bridge. He stood there for a few moments. " Stand by to dive," he said.

Davis stared at him. " We're too far away to dive for an approach, Skipper," he protested.

" You heard me loud and clear," said Currie calmly. " Stand by to dive! "

Mack Davis turned with a scowl on his face. " Look-outs! " he snapped. " Stand by to dive! "

The klaxon blasted below. Bob pulled at his glasses to free them from the railing, but the loop tightened. He fumbled with the jammed knot.

Each lookout descended in front of Lieutenant Davis so that he could see them. " Last man, sir! " said Red Kelly. Commander Currie dropped through the hatch. " Clear the bridge! " roared Lieutenant Davis. " Dive! Dive! Dive! "

Bob started for the hatch, then whirled. He couldn't leave those glasses hanging there. He reached for them and heard the hatch bang shut. The sea began to gush into space already opened by venting compressed air that had partially, or completely filled certain tanks. The diving planes moved and *Grayfin* tilted her blunt bullnose toward the darkness of the depths. Water was rushing swiftly through the freeway beneath the deck superstructure.

Bob yelled at the top of his voice. He dropped the glasses. Water foamed past with a *snick-snick-snick* sound. The sub was lower in the water. The sea was slapping the deckboards from underneath, filling up the freeway, while little plumes and jets of water spurted up through the openings. The deck was already awash.

Bob screamed wildly. In a matter of minutes the sub would drop from beneath him, so to speak, and he'd be

48

alone on that moonlit sea. He ran forward and yelled into the bridge telephone as seawater washed up about his knees. The sub sank lower and the water rose to his thighs. Then *Grayfin,* as though she had heard Bob call out, lurched a little and leveled off. It seemed to Bob as though the bridge deck was pushing up against his feet. The deckboards appeared again, wet and glistening, When the submarine was at surface, moving swiftly along, there was one thoroughly frightened lookout standing there hanging onto a rail. He turned and ripped the glasses free from the railing and hastily wiped them on his shirt.

The hatch popped open with a gushing of air and the face of Commander Currie appeared. He had no expression on his face. " Get below " he said. He pulled himself up onto the bridge deck. Just as he did so, there was a faint sparking of light far across the silvery surface of the sea. As Bob started down the ladder he heard a rushing, whirring sound.

" Dive! Dive! Dive! " roared Commander Currie. His shoes hit Bob atop the head as the officer came down the ladder and slammed shut the hatch. The wheel spun and the *Grayfin* again tilted steeply forward and down. Bob landed on the control room floor all in a heap, still clinging to the glasses that had come so close to causing his death. Any second now the commander would order battle stations submerged, to go in for the attack.

Grayfin was piling tons of seawater over her and yet there was no command from the skipper. Now and then some of the men or officers in the control room glanced quickly at each other. This wasn't at all like Gil Currie.

The skipper spoke, altering the course. The helmsman repeated it and then obeyed the command. *They were*

49

turning sharply away from the oncoming ships! Mack Davis had a face like the approach of a line squall. He was overdue for a boat of his own. Scuttlebutt had it that he was considered too impetuous for command of a boat. Serving time as exec under Gil Currie on *Grayfin* was supposed to calm him down. He wasn't any better fighting man than Gil Currie, but he needed more of Currie's calmness and precision before he got his own command.

The gyrocompass jumped and began swinging jerkily to the right as *Grayfin* swung about. The helmsman skillfully met the swinging needle by responding with the wheel just before the gyro needle hit the new course reading. "Steady on two-three-oh, sir!" said the helmsman.

"Very well," said the skipper. "Hold her there until further orders."

"We're running away," said Mack Davis, as though to himself. He smashed a big fist into his other palm.

"Take it easy, Mack," said Tom Olson, the navigating officer. "Skip knows what he's doing."

"Sound fading away, sir," said the sonarman.

The long white needle on the depth gauge hit eighty feet and kept on going toward ninety. "Level her off," came the command. The skipper came down the ladder from the conning tower. "Take over, Mack," he said. "You've got the conn." He passed through the forward doorway and was gone.

Mack Davis stared at the empty doorway. He looked at Olson. "Can you beat that?" he asked.

Ensign Tolliver rubbed his jaw. He looked from one to the other of the two officers. "Maybe they *were* cruisers," he suggested. "Destroyers anyway. There were three of them, remember."

"We're out here to fight a war," said Davis.

50

Olson shrugged. "There are enlisted men present, Mack," he said. His meaning was plain enough.

Bob faded out of the control room and went aft to the crew's mess. Gary looked at him with wide eyes. "You loco?" he asked fiercely. "If someone hadn't taped the bridge telephone button open, you wouldn't have been heard at all!"

"It was reported that all lookouts were below," said Bob.

Red Kelly looked up from his coffee cup. "You blaming me for your stupidity?" he asked quickly.

All eyes flicked toward Red and then to Bob.

Bob flushed. "No," he said evenly, "but you miscounted, that's all."

Red Kelly stood up. He was shorter than Bob by half a head but he was well proportioned and muscular and several years older than Bob. "You tin can sailors think you're so blasted smart," he said thinly. "On sub duty you jump when you hear a command."

"Don't be a Marine," said Bob coldly. "Whether I jumped or not, you still miscounted."

Red walked forward. Gary smiled uneasily. "Both of you were wrong, fellows," he said. "Apologize."

Red shot a hard look at him. "Keep your big nose out'a this, Skinny," he said, "or you'll get some too."

Gary's face changed. "Belt 'em, pal," he said to Bob.

Chief Daly walked into the messroom. "What's this?" he asked.

Stan Blascovitz smiled. "How about some hot raisin pie, Chief?" he suggested.

"Later," said the chief. "What's going on here?"

"Dunbar says I miscounted," Red explained.

"Kelly says I was too stupid and too slow to get below

51

when we got the command," said Bob.

Daly placed his big hands on his lean hips. "Oh," he said softly.

His meaning was clear enough. *Both* of them had been wrong. He looked about the room. "Now hear this," he said. "Because one greenhorn doesn't know enough to jump and make it so at a command and another man can't count up to four without using his fingers, we nearly lost a man a little while ago. Furthermore, by surfacing again, a Jap got a crack at us. That shell passed right over the top of us. Some of you heard the cracking noise through the open hatch. The skipper risked this boat and the whole crew to surface and save Dunbar's life. I'm not so sure, if I had been skipper if I would have done it with three Jap cruisers or tin cans aheading at flank speed toward us. The next shot might have hit us or we might have caught a full salvo, and the Japs can shoot almost as well at night as they do during daylight. That was too close for comfort."

Baldy shifted his gum. "Maybe so," he said. "But why did we run away?"

Daly turned and looked at him. "Who said we ran away?" he demanded.

"It's pretty obvious, isn't it?" said the motormac.

"Ol' Lootenant Davis was sure burned up," said Slim Polk. He shook his head. "I never seen him so mad since the time he missed the brow coming aboard one dark night at Pearl and fell into the water. You could hear him clear to Diamond Head."

"He's not the skipper," said Blascovitz. "Skip knows what he's doing."

"Not like the old days on *Grayfin*," said Red Kelly. "We used to be a *fighting* ship then. Come into Pearl with a broom lashed to the periscope shears. Three Jap buckets up there and we're hiding out like a rabbit in a cabbage patch."

The speaker on the bulkhead broke into life. " Now hear this! Now hear this! The skipper will speak to all of you." All eyes flicked toward the speaker. The level voice of the commander came through the speaker. " Tonight, because of the slowness of one lookout and the carelessness of another, we not only came close to losing a man, but also endangered the boat. This is not like the crew of the *Grayfin.* Our mission does not allow us to be careless. There seems to be a lack of discipline apparent among some of you. This will not be tolerated." The voice died away.

" Now he'll maybe tell us why he ran away from them tin cans," said Baldy.

" There will be no disciplinary action against the two men who endangered the boat," said the skipper. " But it will not happen again! I repeat. *It will not happen again!* That is all."

They all looked at one another. " Maybe he's turning chicken," said Red Kelly. " Maybe he's got *Maru* fever."

Chief Daly slowly reached out with one big hand, gripped Kelly by the front of his shirt and drew him close, boring into the redhead's eyes with his own hard eyes. " You make a crack like that once more, mister," he said, " and I personally will break you in half." He shoved Kelly back and turned on a heel, leaving the messroom.

The speaker had been left on. " All clear on sound gear, sir," came the voice of Scarlotti.

" Prepare to surface," came the command. The surfacing alarm sounded.

The submarine tilted upward and in a matter of minutes the main induction opened hydraulically. The soft

53

purring of the electric motors stopped and the diesels roared into life one after the other as the ship reached the surface. Air roared into the *Grayfin* as the hatch was opened. Once again Bob raced up the ladder to take his station as lookout. The moon had drifted behind the clouds and the sea was dark except for the sudsy foam streaming back from the prow of *Grayfin* and spreading into a wide frothy wake.

"Permission to start the turboblow," said Ensign Tolliver.

"Permission granted," rasped Mack Davis.

"Permission to charge batteries," said the young officer.

"Permission granted," said Davis. He clenched the lip of the bridge with his big hands and looked forward with a bitter look on his broad face.

Red Kelly glanced down at Bob. "I'm sorry, kid," he said. "I was wrong."

"Forget it, Red," said Bob with a smile. "I *was* too slow. Next time I'll break the boat record."

"Quiet aft there!" roared Davis. "This boat is getting to be full of chatterers and old women! There's a war on out here, but you'd never know it!"

Red looked at Bob. He pointed below. His meaning was clear enough. Davis was referring to the skipper, with his usual bluntness. *Grayfin* was *not* a happy boat.

5

For two hours *Grayfin* had risen to periscope depth every half hour for a look-see. Commander Currie, forehead pressed against the sponge-rubber eyepiece, arms draped over the training handles, would make a 360-degree sweep. Time after time he would command Down scope, slapping the training handles up against the tube, and stepping back as an enlisted man would press the black button that drew the heavy instrument down into its well with a whining of the electric motor and the wire cables that drew it down.

Bob Dunbar stood close to the radar console, watching the screen, although the radar antenna hadn't been out of water for hours, but orders had been given to Radarman Buck Preble to stand by, and while waiting, he had been quietly instructing Bob. It must be almost dawn. The evening before, *Grayfin* had surfaced long enough to recharge batteries and then had dived instead of running on the surface until dawn. Something was in the wind.

Scarlotti, the sonarman, glanced up. "Terrific rain squalls on the surface," he said. "Coming and going. It's foul up there."

"Persicope depth," quietly ordered the skipper.

Grayfin slanted upward. "Up scope," said the skipper. The scope man pressed the white button on the "scope pickle." The scope started up with a whining of cables, Commander Currie squatting to meet it, riding it up. He peered intently through the eyepiece, turning the scope slowly to cover all points of the compass. He nodded to himself, slapped the training handles up against the scope. " Down scope! Stand by to surface! "

The surfacing signal blared out from the klaxon and the crew went into swift action. Bob turned toward the ladder to get ready to go on lookout duty. He picked up his foul-weather jacket and slipped quickly into it, then picked up a pair of binoculars from those atop the gyrocompass table. He swiftly cleaned the lens with lens paper.

Scarlotti twisted the sound gear back and forth. " Rain still pounding down," he said.

" Good surface cover," said Ensign Tolliver.

" For who? " asked Lieutenant Gamble, the torpedo officer.

" Whom," said Tolliver. " Not *who*."

" All right! For *whom?* Us or the Nips? "

" Surface! " snapped Commander Currie. " Lookouts in the conning tower! Shift to all four diesels! All ahead, standard! "

The hatch popped open with a swift rush of air. The low-pressure blowers began a series of squeals in rising pitch as the air returned through the still-revolving fans after the valves had been secured. Bob leaped for the ladder and raced up to meet the draft of fresh salt air that struck his face after the rush of air from the interior of the submarine. As he reached his station the rain slanted down heavily. He turned up the hood of his oilskin jacket. It was dawn. Clouds hung low on the heaving waters. *Grayfin* rolled heavily, burying her nose into the waves, sending up showers of spray that whipped back toward the conning tower. Visibility was narrowed to a few hundred yards in the grayish-yellowish light. Rain squalls swept across the heaving waters in bursts, lashing savagely at the rolling black hull of the submarine. Water broke heavily over the boat, sweeping across the slotted wooden deck to smash against the superstructure. Every now and then a wave would curl up and hurl water onto the bridge, sweeping aft to pour past the periscope shears and radar antenna to flow knee-deep off the cigarette deck.

Despite all his efforts, Bob could not keep the binocular lenses free of the salt spray. Surprisingly enough, the submarine seemed to be a fine sea boat. In fact, she seemed to ride better than a destroyer would have done under the same circumstances, although Bob had to admit the bridge of a destroyer would have been a great deal drier. He glanced up at the revolving radar antenna, wondering if the foul weather would affect the efficiency of the gear. The visual lookouts couldn't be of much value in this type of weather.

Bob remembered how *Logie* had been throttled down during the storm that had swept Bob and Gary from her decks. The 60,000-shaft horsepower had been of little avail in that maelstrom of wind and water. Certainly this storm wasn't anything like the one *Logie* had faced, but Commander Currie was driving *Grayfin* hard into the smashing seas. Running on the surface in daylight in such weather, at such a speed, meant but one thing. *Grayfin* was getting close to the scene of her mission, whatever it was.

Bob glanced toward the bridge. The commander was on deck, clad in oilskins, peering into the flying spray that showered back from the plunging bow. The only consolation was that the enemy would have just as hard a time seeing *Grayfin* in this muck as *Grayfin* would have of seeing them. Radar would do it, but intelligence had reported that the Japanese had but little other than a primitive form of radar, although surprisingly enough, according to Radarman Buck Preble, it had been a Japanese scientist who had developed the directional antenna as far back as 1932.

Grayfin slammed ahead into the heaving seas until Bob went off watch, and still there had been no indication from Commander Currie that he planned to dive. Things were chaotic below. The constant pitching and heaving of the submarine had broken a freshwater pipe, which had partially flooded the crew's quarters. When that had been fixed, a saltwater pipe had broken in the pump room, threatening to flood the forward battery room, which could have been disastrous. Only quick work by Chief Daly and some of the men had stopped the leak in time.

" What's the skipper trying to do? " growled Hank Seitz, the yeoman. " Drive her under? "

Bob filled a coffee cup and balanced himself against the pitching and heaving of the boat. " This is almost as bad as being on a tin can in a storm," he said.

" What's it like up there, pal? " asked Gary from the galley window.

" Foul," said Bob. " Visibility a few hundred yards. Spray and rain flying all over the place. Lookouts aren't much good in this stuff."

Slim Polk braced himself against a bulkhead. " Well," he said resignedly, " wherever we're going, we ought to be getting there."

" We've been under way a long time on this patrol," said Red Kelly, " and we still don't know where we're going."

Bob emptied his cup. " I'm going to get some sack

time," he said. " The way things look, I'll put in another watch on deck before we dive again."

Gary peeled off his apron. "I'll join you," he said. " Cooking and baking is rough work for a man."

" Listen to him," jeered Slim. " He eats more than he cooks. Blas says Lunt doesn't even let the mess break even."

" Jealousy," said Gary loftily.

They worked their way forward, steadying themselves as *Grayfin* pitched and rolled. Something smashed to the deck. A tool bounced from a shelf and missed Bob by inches.

They climbed into their bunks, listening to the creaking and groaning of the hull and to the smashing of the seas against her bows. Now and then *Grayfin* plunged deeply and it seemed as if she never would come up. Bob eyed the huge, heavy torpedoes in their slings, moving a little uneasily with the motion of the submarine. He closed his eyes. He was almost getting used to submarine life, and if it hadn't been for the mystery that shrouded *Grayfin's* mission, he would actually have been enjoying the different experience.

Once or twice, during his rest, he awakened, only to experience the same rough motion of the boat, by which he knew they were still on the surface and moving into the teeth of the storm, all ahead, standard. He glanced toward Gary's bunk, and saw that he was fast asleep, one arm thrown comfortably over his bunkie, about eighteen feet of cylindrical steel weighing about three thousand pounds containing about six hundred pounds of highly explosive torpex, or TPX. Bob grinned and dropped off to sleep again, bracing himself against the pitching and rolling of *Grayfin*.

59

A hand shook Bob awake. He looked up into the smiling face of Dusty Fuller. " Time for watch, pal," he said, still smiling.

" Already? "

The boy nodded. " You've got about fifteen minutes to get ready. Grab a cup of joe. It's cold up there."

" Still on the surface? Have we cut down speed? "

" Nope. The old *Grayfin* is taking a beating but we're in a hurry to get *somewhere*."

Bob threw back his blanket and reached for his shoes. " Is it raining, Dusty? " he asked.

The boy shook his head. " Only now and then we plow through a light squall. Hardly enough to bother about, but you'd better take your foul-weather gear." He leaned back and hung on to a stanchion as *Grayfin* plunged deeply. " Man, if I let go, I'll tumble all the way down into the maneuvering room."

Grayfin arose, shaking herself like a dog throwing off water from its coat. Down she went again, deep, deep, and then she arose spasmodically, throwing herself to one side. As she did so, there was a sound like a pistol shot, followed by another and another. Bob looked about. *Grayfin* dived deeply and as she arose a torpedo sagged in its lashings and began to slide aft. " Look out, Dusty! " he screamed.

The huge cylinder slid slowly out of its lashings. Some of the broken leather slings hung down. Another torpedo popped like a pistol and slid swiftly toward the boy. Dusty let go of the stanchion and ran aft toward the door. The torpedo was too fast for him. It smashed its tail across the washbowl, falling heavily sideways, partially atop the boy who went down below it. *Grayfin* pitched down, and the massive cylinder slid forward, ramming its rounded war-

60

head with frightful force against the brass door of a torpedo tube.

"Jam it!" yelled Gary from his bunk. He hurled his blankets atop the torpedo. Blankets and pillows rained down as men awoke in their bunks and helped Gary. The torpedo seemed jammed against a stanchion. Bob slid from his bunk and dropped aft to where Dusty lay helplessly. He gripped the boy under the armpits and pulled him through the door as the torpedo slid aft again, shattering the washbowl. Water spurted from a broken line. Bob dragged the unconscious boy into the wardroom.

"What's this?" yelled Ensign Tolliver.

"Torpedo broke loose, sir!" said Bob. "Fuller is badly hurt."

"Get the doc!" snapped the officer. "Send for the chief torpedoman! Tell bridge to slow down until we get that torp under control!"

Bob raced aft to obey his instructions. *Grayfin* was eased off. A scratch crew made the torpedo fast. Pharmacist's Mate First Class Royal Duryea looked up into Commander Currie's set white face and shook his head.

"Can't you do anything?" asked the skipper.

Duryea stood up. "He's all smashed up inside," he said softly. He closed his eyes and looked aside.

Dusty opened his eyes and smiled up into Bob's face. "Don't forget to wear your foul-weather gear," he said clearly. "It's wet up there." He closed his eyes.

The pharmacist bent over the slim body for a moment or two. He reached for a blanket and pulled it up over the smiling face. "It had to be him," he said quietly.

A chain hoist rattled in the forward torpedo room. In a few minutes Chief Torpedoman Potter came into the wardroom. "All secure, sir," he said to the skipper.

"How did it happen, Chief?" asked the skipper.

"There was a flaw in one of the slings. Ordinarily it would have held, but the motion of the boat worked on it. When it broke, the strain was too much for the others. It wasn't anyone's fault, sir."

Currie nodded. He walked aft out of the wardroom.

"No one's fault?" said Gary bitterly. "If he hadn't been trying to drive *Grayfin* under, the lashing would have held."

"Stow that, Mac!" growled Potter.

Bob looked at the chief torpedoman. He knew that Potter agreed with Gary. The pharmacist stood and looked down at Dusty's still form. "He just turned eighteen the other day," he said. "This was the beginning of his second year of service. He's listed as being nineteen, but he wasn't that old."

Potter wiped the sweat from his face. "He's an only child too," he said.

Power throbbed through the hull of the submarine as speed was picked up again, and the submarine drove on into the teeth of the storm. The body began to roll to one side. Bob dropped onto his knees and held it. It had been such a short time ago that the boy had awakened Bob with that wonderful smile of his.

"What happens now?" said Gary.

"It was an accident, Gary," said the pharmacist.

Gary looked down at the boy. "I mean, what do we do with *him?*"

The chief torpedoman examined a cut on his hand. He did not look up as he spoke. "You've been in this man's Navy long enough to know," he said quietly.

"Dunbar!" snapped Chief Daly from the doorway. "You're due on watch! Now!"

Bob turned on a heel. He hurried to the control room and up the ladder to take his post in the gray, drizzling world of the open sea. He was glad of one thing: everyone on deck watch had a face wet with salt spray. It was hard to tell if some of the salt was tears. The eyes told the story. There was a sick hurt in most of them.

But a submarine on patrol deep in enemy territory must keep on functioning no matter what happens aboard it. The rain had eased off, and although the sea was still heaving at dusk, there was a faint suggestion of moonlight coming through the rifts of the ragged overcast.

Grayfin's engines were stopped. The slight body, wrapped in canvas, was carried up onto the wet, rolling deck. An American flag covered the body. Those who could not come up on deck listened to the speakers as Commander Currie read the burial service. " 'We therefore commit his body to the deep, looking for the general Resurrection in the last day and the life of the world to come, through our Lord Jesus Christ; at whose second coming in glorious majesty to judge the world, the sea shall give up her dead. . . . Let us pray.' " The crew, both those on deck and within the submarine, repeated the Lord's Prayer. The weighted body slid into the gray sea, the flag being held back. The flag was carefully folded and it was then handed to Commander Currie by Chief Daly.

"All those not on watch clear the deck!" said Commander Currie. "Start all four diesels. All ahead, standard."

The tinkling of the engine annunciators sounded. The four engines roared into life, spitting loud blasts from the exhausts. The combined strength of sixty-four cylinders pushing twin screws drove the submarine on into the heaving seas. The moonlight had appeared just long enough to bury the dead. It disappeared behind the clouds. Rain slanted mistily down from the overcast. Once again *Grayfin* forged on to her unknown mission in enemy waters.

6

GRAYFIN had dived just before the dawn, sinking to come to rest on the soft bottom. The depth gauge needle had stopped at 150. There were few human sounds in the submarine; only mechanical noises broke the quiet. Most of the crew were in their bunks, resting in order to conserve the use of air. But it was hot and muggy, hard to breathe and difficult to sleep. Water condensed and dripped down the inside of the conning tower.

The crew had been ordered to stay quiet, but that couldn't stop them from thinking. They knew to a man they were deep into enemy territory, but they didn't know *where* they were. Perhaps it would have been better to know, and perhaps not. They had been on the way for days on this patrol and yet in all that time *Grayfin* had not used her teeth or claws. Not a torpedo had been fired. The deck gun was unused.

It was a chance for coaching if nothing else. Bob Dunbar was watching Scarlotti, the sonarman, with the permission of Chief Daly. The sonar was the ears of *Grayfin,* as the radar was useless. Bob heard a humming, vibrating noise in the earphones, but the sonarman did not move. He spoke out of the side of his mouth. " Fish traffic," he said quietly. Bob wondered how a sonarman could differentiate one sound from another, but Scarlotti was good at it. It sounded like static at times to Bob, and at other times like the noises of propellers, and at times like a Bronx cheer, as though the fish were laughing at the steel monster that had come into their domain and was afraid to move around like a *real* fish.

An expert sonarman could, by listening to propeller beats, estimate speed, range, type of ship, and what it was doing, but to Bob the sounds he heard through the earphones were a hopeless confusion. Bob jumped and tore the phones from his ears as something jarred through the listening device. He clapped his hands to his ears. Scarlotti had winced at the jarring noise. "Crazy old fish whacked his head against the sound head," he said to Bob. He held up a hand and shook his head. Bob replaced the earphones. A faint *thrum-thrum-thrum* sounded through the phones. Bob was experienced enough by now to know it was the sound of something besides fish traffic. The sound grew louder and louder. "Sound contact!" said Scarlotti.

Bob looked at the long white needle of the depth gauge. He would have felt a great deal better with more water piled atop the motionless *Grayfin*.

Scarlotti listened intently. "High-speed screws," he said.

The sound was more of a roaring noise now, and then it died slowly away, but still remained in the background. "Bearing three-three-oh," said the sonarman. "Ship is pinging."

There was no question about the nationality of the ship that was *pinging*, echo-ranging for whatever lay below the surface of the water. The pinging came regularly through the earphones. Cold sweat broke out on Bob as he listened. It was as though a ghost was feeling through the water for the unseen submarine.

Ensign Tolliver was junior officer of the deck. He switched on the speaker that would carry the sound of echo-ranging to the crew. The steady *pinging* at two- to three-minute intervals carried throughout the listening submarine. Somehow it was better that way. As long as it was *ping-g-g-g*, the sonic wave from the Japanese A/S vessel on the surface wasn't striking anything, but if it changed to *poing-g-g-g*, the A/S vessel was picking up an echo.

The sound slowly died away. The fish traffic began again, intermingled with other noises, like a soft frying sound. Scarlotti made a complete sweep with the apparatus. He looked up at Bob. "Sometimes an A/S craft picks up wrecks, or something like that, but if they happen to know these waters well enough, they have them thoroughly charted."

Bob nodded. "Obviously," he said, "but we don't *know* where we are."

"Tokyo Bay," said the sonarman.

"You've got a great sense of humor, Scarlotti," said Ensign Tolliver.

The faint thrum-thrum-thrum came again. "High-speed screws," said the sonarman. "Bearing two-seven-oh. Wait! There's another one. Bearing three-two-oh."

"Great," murmured Tolliver. "Maybe the first one thinks he's located something." He spoke into the speaker. "Not a sound out of any of you! Stop breathing if you can."

Bob knew what Tolliver meant. Any sound at all seemed highly magnified. If a tool was dropped, the sound could easily be picked up.

The sound of the screws came louder and louder until with a vicious-sounding *chow-chow-chow*, the A/S vessel

67

passed right over the *Grayfin* and the sound filled the interior of the submarine. It faded away for a time. Then the echo-ranging started again, this time from a bearing directly astern of the submerged *Grayfin*.

"They're sure feeling around," said Chief Daly as he came into the control room. "Officers' meeting is breaking up in the wardroom, sir," he said to Ensign Tolliver.

The young officer looked at the chief of the boat. "What do you think, Daly?" he asked.

Daly shrugged. "I think the skipper busted open those secret orders."

"You're right," a dry voice said. Commander Currie came into the control room. "You'll all hear them in a minute." He listened to the echo-ranging in the speaker. "Dying away, eh, Scarlotti?" he added.

"I can only pick up one of them now, sir," said the sonarman.

Minutes slowly ticked past and then it was quiet, at least as far as the searching A/S vessels were concerned. Maybe it was only a routine patrol. The speaker that carried the sound of the sonar apparatus was switched off and the skipper took over. "Now hear this, *Grayfin*," said the submarine commander. "I have opened and read the instructions given to me prior to our sailing on this mission. All I had prior to this time was a location to reach, which we have done. Our mission is twofold. We are just off Sibutu Passage and off the Sulu Archipelago between the Tawitawi Group and North Borneo."

Scarlotti's eyes met those of Bob. The thick, dark eyebrows went up. Sibutu Passage was just off the Celebes Sea, and led into the Sulu Sea, and beyond the Sulu Sea was Balabac Strait that led into the South China Sea. There was something else that came to Bob's memory.

Tawitawi, or Tawi Tawi, began ringing a bell in Bob's mind.

"Our primary mission," continued the skipper, "is to pick up a team of British and Australian commandos who have been operating behind the Japanese lines in these waters for the past two years. Their information is of vital importance to the Allied forces operating in the Pacific. Three attempts have already been made by submarines to pick them up. All of them failed. This time they picked the right boat. *Grayfin* will *not* fail."

"Sound contact, sir," said the sonarman. "High-speed screws again. Bearing two-seven-oh. Coming fast."

Commander Currie nodded. "Echo-ranging. Very likely the regular patrol. There are quite a few wrecks in these waters from the early part of the war. The Japs don't know we are here, but they may suspect we will attempt to get the commandos off."

"She's moving away," said Scarlotti. "Echo-ranging again."

"Once we get the commandos off," said the skipper, "there is one other part of our mission. We are to scout the major Japanese Fleet Operating Base at Tawitawi. We are more likely to be spotted then than we are now, but we must get the commandos off within the next forty-eight hours if we can. If we can't . . ." His voice trailed off.

"Contact is gone, sir," said Scarlotti.

Commander Currie shoved back his hat and wiped the sweat from his forehead. "Now you know, men, why we were in such a hurry to get here and remained undetected. We have reached close to the rendezvous at the right time. The rest is up to you and *Grayfin*. That is all." He flipped off the speaker switch.

The air became fouler as *Grayfin* waited for the dark-

69

ness that would conceal her surfacing in narrow Sibutu Passage. She would have to run in on the surface that night, and if those busy Japanese A/S craft were still about, it would be a perilous game of hide-and-seek between them and *Grayfin*. One mistake and *Grayfin* would have it.

Grayfin was at last raised to periscope depth, with Commander Currie making a periscope sweep. There had been no indication of A/S or other surface craft on the sonar gear. It was very quiet except for the mechanical noises of the boat, the interlaced mutterings of bow and stern motors working to adjust the *Grayfin's* keel to the ordered depth, tanks gurgling water.

"Dark as the inside of a boot," said the skipper. "Turn on that sonar, Scarlotti."

The sonarman flipped a switch. Fish-traffic noises and the faint gurgling of the tanks threaded through the sound of the bow and stern motors. If *Grayfin* heard screws approaching, she would have to dive fast. The depth gauge needle hung at periscope depth. The fathometer showed 125 feet beneath the boat's keel, hardly enough water to help hold off a depth-charging.

Slowly, ever so slowly, *Grayfin* moved into the passage, with the lone eye of the periscope peering into the darkness, dependent on one man, the sonarman, for safety, such as it was in those enemy-infested waters.

Commander Currie had said three submarines had already failed on this mission. *How* had they failed? The thought raced through Bob's mind. He remembered all too well what Tokyo Rose had said one night about *Grayfin's* leaving Brisbane for duty in the Central Pacific and that the *Logie* had been lost at sea in a typhoon. She had also known about *Corvina's* being lost as well as *Sculpin*. If she

70

had known about *Grayfin's* being sent to the Central Pacific on patrol duty, might she not have also known where *Grayfin* was going? Maybe the rest of *Grayfin's* crew might accept that intense A/S echo-ranging activity while *Grayfin* lay submerged at the mouth of Sibutu Passage, but it had seemed a lot more personal to Bob.

" Stand by to surface! " said the skipper. He swung the scope again. " Down scope! " He slapped up the handles and stepped back as the periscope slid down into its deep well with a whining of cables.

Bob snatched up a pair of night glasses from the gyro-compass table. The other lookouts filed into the control room. Commander Currie was not ordering the deck guns to be manned. He had no intention of fighting on the surface if they were surprised, but on the other hand, there was hardly enough water under *Grayfin's* keel for a deep enough dive to get away from a severe depth-charging.

" Lookouts! Stand by to surface! " came the command.

The surfacing alarm sounded, and the boat tilted upward. The hatch was cracked and a spray of water dripped down and then was whipped back upward again as air rushed out of the boat from one end to the other, carrying papers and other odds and ends with it. A globule of bluish air poured out of the open hatch into the darkness of the night.

Bob was up the ladder and at his post, inhaling deep lungfuls of the fresh, tropical air. It was pitch-dark, but there was a faint line of white foam rushing back on either side of the bows to form a wider wake behind the submarine. *Grayfin* was moving at slow speed in order not to make too much noise, but the sound of the exhausts and the rushing of the wake seemed loud enough to Bob to alert anyone within a mile or so of the submarine.

He swung the night glasses about, but there was nothing to be seen. The radar whirred as it moved about, covering the darkness that seemed to flow in on top of *Grayfin*. God help the submarine if radar or sonar failed in their duty tonight, for visibility from the deck of the submarine was practically nil.

There would be a moon later on. Bob wondered what the skipper would do then. The black-painted *Grayfin* would stand out on the silvery waters like a sore thumb. Somewhere in the darkness would be the A/S craft, feeling out with their echo-ranging for American submarines, and with their radar antenna spinning about. Rumor had it that the Japanese didn't have radar, or that it was inaccurate and of extremely short range, but in the confined waters of Sibutu Passage it wouldn't have to be of long range.

Bob heard the bridge speaker squawk, but he couldn't distinguish any words. The annunciators tinkled and the roaring of the diesels stopped. The submarine rolled easily in the chop, drifting with the current.

Red Kelly looked down at Bob. "Radar picked up a plane," he said tersely.

The plane couldn't hear the sound of *Grayfin's* engines, but it might pick up the spreading wake of the submarine. The faint humming sound of the engine came to the quiet submarine. Slowly and steadily the plane moved down the length of the passage, passing almost directly over the submarine. Then the sound faded away. There were no other warnings from the bridge squawk box. The annunciators tinkled softly, and *Grayfin* moved on into the darkness at about four knots.

The moonlight appeared about the time Bob's watch came to an end, but by this time the submarine had moved in close to a low headland where the water was comparatively deep, and it lay there gently rolling until the batteries were fully charged. A plane or an A/S vessel would not be able to hear the low humming of the diesel engine charging the battery above the sound of their own engines.

When the moon was fully up, *Grayfin* sank to the bottom of the passage in barely ninety feet of clear water. There was no need to warn the crew to remain extra quiet. They all knew well enough that they were in a precarious position and would be until they had picked up the commandos and headed for the Celebes Sea with plenty of water beneath them.

Bob was in the messroom devouring a tuna salad sandwich, made by the expert hands of Gary Lunt, when the speaker on the bulkhead sounded off.

" Now hear this, *Grayfin*," came the voice of the skipper. "We will remain submerged until sometime tomorrow, and then move in for a periscope reconnaissance of the bay where we are supposed to pick up the commandos. At dusk we will land our personal commandos to contact the Australians. We hope to contact them right away, but if we don't pick them up several hours before dawn, *Grayfin* will leave the bay and submerge for the day, to return to the rendezvous again at dusk. It will be up to our contact party to remain on shore until we do pick up the commandos." There was a short pause. " There is not much need to tell you that Sibutu Passage is constantly patrolled by A/S craft, as well as plane patrols. What you should know is that the bay area is well patrolled by foot soldiers. Only the most experienced of you will be able to avoid them if it is necessary to remain ashore for an additional sixteen or seventeen hours."

There were half a dozen crewmen in the messroom.

They looked up at the speaker and then sideways out of the corners of their eyes at their shipmates.

" Chief Potter will lead our contact party. It will consist of two rubber boats, with walkie-talkie contact between them and *Grayfin*. There will be three men in each boat. We will need an experienced signalman with the party for visual signaling if it is necessary."

Gary Lunt lowered a cup of coffee from his mouth and looked at Bob. Memories flooded back into Bob's mind. Of the days when he and Gary had worked ashore, after losing their PT boat, with Sub-Lieutenant Miles Tierney, of the Royal Australian Navy Volunteer Reserve, as volunteer coast watchers, until weakness and illness from an old wound had completely incapacitated Tierney and Gary and Bob had taken over, running from Japanese patrols and natives friendly to Japan. When Bob had returned aboard a destroyer for sea duty he had sworn no one would ever get him ashore in the green hell of those tropical islands.

" We have enough volunteers to replace our crew commandos we lost at Brisbane, but unfortunately we can hardly spare a man from his duties aboard *Grayfin*, if we are to avoid the enemy patrols until we complete this mission."

Bob emptied his coffee cup and stood up. Chief Potter looked curiously at him. Gary swallowed hard. He knew what was coming.

" All members of the contact party and volunteers report to the wardroom," continued the skipper. " That is all."

" I knew it," said Gary under his breath.

" They need a signalman," said Bob.

" Does it have to be *you*? " said Gary fiercely.

74

"Are you a signalman, Dunbar?" asked Chief Potter.

"Yes, Chief," said Bob.

"The best," boasted Gary. Then his face changed as he realized what he had said.

"You volunteering?" asked the chief.

"Yes," said Bob quickly before he could change his mind. "I need more fresh air than I can get in a sub."

"That's one way of putting it," said Potter dryly. "Come on then."

"You'll never learn," said Baldy Carter to Bob. He shook his head. "That skinny pal of yours has got more sense than to volunteer."

As Bob followed the chief from the messroom, Gary stripped off his apron and handed it to Blascovitz through the galley window. "Keep this handy for me, Blas," he said. "I'll need it in a couple of days."

Baldy rolled his eyes upward. "Twenty years in this man's Navy and I never volunteered yet."

"Proud of yourself, eh?" said Blascovitz scornfully.

Half a dozen men were in the wardroom when Potter entered, followed by Bob and Gary. Commander Currie looked up. "You two destroyermen are not members of the crew," he said. "No need to get mixed up in this."

"We're also members of the United States Navy, sir," said Bob.

The skipper nodded. "You're a signalman, aren't you?"

"Second Class, sir," said Bob.

"What about you, Lunt?" said Commander Currie.

"Gunner's Mate Third Class, sir." Gary smiled. "Me and Dunbar work well together."

"I heard about those Silver Stars," said the officer.

Gary flushed. "We were lucky, sir."

"I'm not so sure about that."

75

Bob looked about. He saw Slim Polk, Red Kelly, and Joe Krasnowski. Chief Daly leaned against a bulkhead beside two other crewmen whom Bob knew slightly.

The skipper looked at Chief Potter. "Chief Daly wants to lead the shore party, Potter," he said.

"It's my duty, sir," said Potter.

"They need you on the *Grayfin* more than they do me at this time," said Daly.

The commander glanced at the chief of the boat. "Do you feel up to it, Daly? If you do, I'd rather have you go."

"Never felt better in my life."

Bob looked away from the older man. What was Daly trying to prove?

"Lunt and Dunbar have volunteered, sir," said Potter.

"That will make the six men we need," Currie said. He looked at the two men beside Daly. "Stein and Miller," he said, "you are excused. Thanks for the offer."

The two men seemed to have a look of relief on their faces as they left the wardroom.

Daly looked at Potter. "You didn't know this," he said quietly, "but this is my last war patrol. I got my orders just before leaving Brisbane. I'm heading for New London as an instructor when we get back from this patrol."

"Couldn't have picked a better man," said Potter.

"This is my last real chance for a little action," said Daly.

"I understand," said the torpedoman. He was obviously disappointed. He smiled. "I've got work to do as long as I'm not mixed up in this thing."

"Go ahead, Potter," said the skipper.

It was very quiet in the wardroom except for the humming of an electric motor. "We'll need coffee, Kelly," said the skipper. "Sit down, men. We'll go over the chart of

76

the bay and the lay of the land. Your gear is all ready. I hope you two can swim well," he said to Bob and Gary.

" I thought we had rubber boats, sir," Gary said.

" Two," said the skipper. " But you never know."

Bob glanced at Gary. Memories came flooding back again, but it was too late to do anything now. For better or for worse they were committed to the landing party, but neither of them had expected to serve under Chief Daly.

7

DURING the hours of darkness after the dying of the moon *Grayfin* had moved at dead slow speed submerged into the shallow approaches to the bay where the rendezvous was to be made, then had settled to the soft bottom. During the hours of bright daylight careful periscope reconnaissance had been made of the shore with its white sand and waving mangrove trees. Commander Currie had called each of the shore party to the periscope to make them as familiar as possible with the area. It appeared to be a pleasant summer resort. Twice during the day Japanese patrols had been seen slogging through the sand.

At regular intervals the *Grayfin*'s sonar had picked up high-speed screws and echo-ranging out in Sibutu Passage, but none of the A/S craft ventured near the sub. The major problem was that patrol planes might easily sight the black hull of the submarine in the clear, shallow waters.

At dusk, before the rising of the moon, *Grayfin* surfaced and ran closer inshore on her electric motors. The six contact men came up onto the deck, clad in dark clothing, with blackened faces, armed with automatic pistols and sheath knives. Chief Daly carried a tommy gun and big Joe Krasnowski carried a Browning automatic rifle. The boats were inflated and lowered into the dark waters for testing. Joe Krasnowski, Red Kelly, and Slim Polk got into one of them and Chief Daly got into the other with Gary and Bob. Each boat had a walkie-talkie radio. The shore was nothing but a mass of thicker darkness and in the silence the faint washing of the surf was heard on the beach. Another sound drifted through the quiet. It was that of a gasoline engine somewhere out in the darkness of Sibutu Passage.

" Fishing boat," said Commander Currie.

" Any of them have radar or echo-ranging gear? " asked Chief Daly.

" Some of the bigger ones," said Lieutenant Davis. " They won't be able to pick up those floating bathtubs you're going ashore in, Daly."

" I wasn't thinking of us," said the chief quietly.

Bob looked toward what he thought was the shore. During darkness everything seemed different, including his usually excellent sense of sight and feeling of direction.

" The moon will be up in a few hours," said the skipper.

" We'll be well under cover by then," said Joe Krasnowski.

" I'll surface at two-hour intervals after the moon is gone," said the skipper, " starting at 2300 hours. If I don't get your signal by one hour before dawn, I'm going back out into the deeper water of the passage."

A cold feeling came over Bob with the skipper's words. The idea of spending a whole day hidden on that shore wasn't exactly appealing.

" Sound contact," rasped the bridge speaker. " Slow-running screws. Bearing one-eight-oh. No echo-ranging."

" Fisherman," said the skipper.

" We *hope*," said Lieutenant Olson. He raised a pair of night glasses and looked out into the thick darkness in the general direction indicated by the sonar contact.

"Plane overhead, sir," said the port lookout.

"Lots of business tonight," said Mack Davis.

"Reflectors all rigged, sir," said Radarman Bader from one of the rubber boats. Thin masts stuck up from each of the boats, supported by wires. These were special reflectors designed by Bader to keep track of the boats by radar as they moved in to the distant and unseen beach.

"Slow ahead on the electric motors," said the skipper.

The annunciators tinkled and *Grayfin* moved dead slow through the dark waters with a leadsman stationed at the bow. "By the mark, six," came back the soft voice of the leadsman.

"We're drawing sixteen feet at this trim, sir," said Lieutenant Olson.

"Aye, aye," said Commander Currie.

"By the deep, five," came back the voice of the leadsman.

"All stop," said the skipper.

The *Grayfin* drifted slowly forward with the momentum. The lapping of the water sounded along her black sides.

"Sonar contact fading away, sir," spoke the bridge speaker.

"Patrol plane moving out over the passage," said a lookout.

"And a half, four!" came the call of the leadsman.

"All back one," said the skipper.

The propellers spun briefly, halting the forward motion of the submarine. "All stop," said the skipper. *Grayfin* lay dead in the water.

Daly looked up from the first boat. "All set, sir," he said softly.

"Cast off then," said Commander Currie. "Good luck!"

Bob picked up the walkie-talkie and pressed the button as Chief Daly and Gary paddled away from the black, salt-encrusted flank of the submarine. "Junior to Papa," he said. "Testing." "Papa to Junior," tinnily answered the speaker. "I read you loud and clear. Good luck, kid."

The boats were big and hard to paddle, but there was a slight inshore set toward the beach more than a thousand yards away, but between the submarine and the shore were rock pinnacles and reefs, almost impossible to see in the darkness.

Half an hour drifted past. The walkie-talkie sounded off in Bob's boat. "This is Papa," said the speaker. "Radar reports you drifting to starboard toward a reef. Correct your course. Steer twenty degrees to the left of your present course."

"Junior reporting," said Bob. "Wilco." He could hear the soft voice of Slim Polk speaking into his walkie-talkie in the other boat about twenty feet behind them. It was pretty quiet except for the washing of the distant surf, and then Bob caught another sound much closer. It was the breaking of water over some obstacle and he knew well enough what that obstacle was. It was razor-sharp coral just below, or perhaps even with the dark surface of the water. If they had hit that . . .

The sound of the plane came again as it swung to follow the line of the dark passage. It was heading away from the mouth of the bay where *Grayfin* floated on the surface.

Forty-five minutes drifted past. Sweat dripped from Bob's blackened face as he thrust with the paddle, feeling a blister form on his right hand. "Some night for a boat ride," he grunted.

"Hush!" hissed Chief Daly. "Stop paddling!"

They drifted slowly through the darkness. Bob strained

81

his eyes. He could hear the surf but he couldn't see a thing.

"Breakers ahead," said Gary suddenly. Trust him to spot the shore first.

Daly looked at Bob. "Tell Papa we're going in. The other boat will hold off until we flash a recognition signal."

Bob pressed the button. "Junior going in," he said. "Tell Sis to wait for recognition signal."

Slowly they moved into the breaking surf, rising and falling, with an occasional dash of spray coming up into the boat. "Now!" snapped Daly. They paddled with all their strength, forcing the unwieldy hulk of the boat into the breakers. She hung sideways for a moment, then swirled under the impetus of desperate paddling and thudded heavily onto the strand. In an instant all three of them were over the side, rushing the boat up beyond the surf. They dropped flat, drawing their pistols. They peered into the velvety darkness while the rich, fruity odors of the foliage, mingled with a taint of rotting vegetation, drifted toward them from the thick jungle that touched the edge of the white sands.

"Stay here," whispered the chief. He bellied off into the darkness.

The surf hissed up on the beach and then withdrew with a dragging sound. The wind waved the trees and brush and it seemed as though the jungle moved a little closer to Bob and Gary lying flat on the damp sand beside the hulking boat.

Minutes ticked past before a soft whistle sounded. Daly bellied across the sand. "All clear," he said. "Let's deflate the boat and get it under cover. That jungle is thick enough to hide *Grayfin*."

The air hissed out of the boat aided by the weight of

the three of them and they hauled it into the brush fifty feet from the beach. Vines and creepers tore at them as they sweated the boat into position and covered it as best they could.

" Signal in Sis," said Daly to Bob.

Bob took the blinker tube and crawled back to the beach. He signaled out into the darkness. As he did so he heard the roaring of the plane. He snapped out the light. He could vaguely make out Sis being driven in through the surf. It landed heavily. " Deflate it! " said Bob. " Get it under cover! That plane is coming in this way! "

The sweating men opened the valve and fell onto the boat to drive the air from it. Gary and Chief Daly came to help them. Suddenly there was a flash of white light in the sky over the bay and an enemy parachute flare blossomed out, shedding a ghastly light over the dark-green jungle and the rippling water of the bay. Bob kept his face turned away from the sky, peering out toward the bay. There was no sign of *Grayfin*. She had vanished back into the depths of the passage just in time.

The flare drifted slowly with the wind. Not a man moved on the beach, although it seemed as though the dark bulk of the rubber boat and the dark-clad men lying around it would be clearly apparent on the white sands. The flare died out and darkness filled in where the light had been.

" Move! " said Daly harshly.

They hauled the boat into the thick brush and hid it. The roaring of the plane faded away. Now and then they could see the blue exhaust flames. The plane disappeared beyond the high hills on a course for the Asian mainland.

" You think he saw that blinker light? " said Krasnowski as he wiped off his automatic rifle.

"Who knows?" growled the chief. "At least he didn't see *Grayfin*." He stood up and slung his tommy gun. "The rendezvous is half a mile north of here in a small cove. Lunt and Dunbar will come with me. The rest of you lay low here with the boats. We ought to be under cover there before the moon comes up. If we locate the Aussies, we'll bring them back here after the moon is gone, and hope we can get out to *Grayfin* before dawn." He turned and plunged off into the clinging brush, heading for the beach.

They walked close to the trees at the edge of the beach. Every so often they stopped to listen, but there was no sound other than the heavy washing of the surf and the moaning of the warm wind through the trees.

There was a faint trace of moonlight when the trio reached the cove. They lay flat in the brush and peered across the dark waters of the cove. There was no sign of life there. Chief Daly rested his head on his thick forearms. "Take a look-see, Dunbar," he said huskily.

"What's wrong, Chief?" asked Gary.

"Nothing! You take a look along the beach, but stay out of the moonlight!"

Gary looked at Bob over the chief and shrugged. Bob shook his head and faded into the brush. The mingled noises of the jungle drifted in around him, faint squeakings and rustlings. There was an odor of rotting vegetation and suddenly he walked knee-deep into a sluggish stream that meandered through the thick growth to form the cove at the edge of the dark bay.

He pushed his way through the rank growth until he found a log that had fallen across the stream. It was soft and rotten but strong enough to support his weight. He walked across it and entered the jungle on the far side and found himself on a clearly defined pathway. He stopped and looked about. There had been no mention of a road or pathway on this side of the bay.

He eased his automatic from the holster, drew back the slide to load it, letting the slide drive forward to place a cartridge in the chamber, then he pushed up the safety. The moonlight was stronger now, sending faint light down through the interlacing branches overhead. Bob padded toward the cove. Suddenly he stopped. There was something dark amid the trees. It looked like something man-made. He crouched low and got into the cover of the trees, then made his way forward again. The moonlight revealed a large shack, built partly of trees and partly of corrugated galvanized iron, long gone to rust.

Nothing had been said about any building on this side of the bay. There were some on the other side, but this side was supposed to be completely deserted. He worked his way through the brush and peered into a window of the shack, but saw nothing. Something squeaked under-foot, and he jumped aside as an animal scuttled over his feet and plunged into the brush. He worked his way along-side the shack with upraised pistol and then saw the moon-light shining on the waters of the cove. There was a point of land that jutted into the cove, thickly covered with trees and brush, but a pathway had been cut through it and it looked as though it had been used quite recently.

Bob squatted in the brush. Surely this was not the place where the commandos were supposed to meet the shore party from *Grayfin*. This would have been a little too ob-vious. He rubbed his jaw and started along the pathway. There were six commandos to be picked up, four Austra-lians and two Britishers. He paused in the shadows of the trees to listen. Faintly, ever so faintly, he heard the sound of an engine coming from somewhere to his right, either along the northern shore of the big bay or perhaps on the bay itself. It could be either a truck or a boat, but the pathways he had followed hadn't been wide enough for a truck or a car.

Bob peered around a thick-trunked tree. Four buildings, in much better shape than the shack he had seen, stood there in the growing moonlight. A rather well built wharf ran out into the cove. A dugout canoe had been pulled up on the shore and it was half full of water.

The sound of the engine came closer. Bob peered through a tangle of brush and saw a faint light moving slowly into the mouth of the cove. It was a boat, all right. Perhaps local fishermen coming into their camp. Then a thought struck him. There had been no mention as to *how* the commandos would get to the rendezvous.

Maybe they had stolen a boat to come to the bay. The situation was touch and go as it was, with delicate timing. One mistake and the whole thing would be off, or perhaps discovered by the Japanese.

The engine slowed down. The moonlight struck full on the boat. It was a large sampan type, so common in Asiatic waters, clumsy-looking, seemingly crudely made, but amazingly strong and seaworthy. The Japanese used them with good effect wherever they went. Bob moved out onto the point of land and dropped flat on the ground, peering through the brush toward the boat that was now slowly approaching the wharf. There were a number of men on the deck of the boat, at least four or five of them. There were supposed to be six commandos to meet the shore party.

The engine was cut to idling speed and the boat drifted in toward the moonlit wharf. One of the men leaped ashore to make the boat fast. Bob could see him clearly.

86

This was no tall, lean Australian, or solid Britisher. It was a Japanese soldier, with putteed legs, khaki-colored clothing, and an odd-looking little fatigue cap. As the boat swung close to and then grated heavily against the wharf, man after man came ashore until there were at least eighteen or twenty of them standing there with grounded rifles. Before Bob could make for the pathway, they started off at a jog trot down the wharf and toward the buildings. He ran silently through the trees, but the Japanese were moving faster than he anticipated and on clearer ground. He dropped flat and rolled beneath some brush as they trotted past him, not ten feet away. Several of them had turned aside toward the buildings. As Bob watched the column, it vanished down the pathway.

Cold sweat soaked through his shirt. They were between him and his two companions. A light flared up in one of the buildings. He could hear some of them talking on the sampan as it rocked gently against the pier.

He stood up and walked toward the path, freezing next to a tree as one of the men came out of the building and looked toward the pathway as though he had heard or seen something. What if they found Chief Daly, or Gary Lunt walked right into them?

There was no choice for it. He couldn't risk the pathway. He forced his way through the tangle as quietly as possible. He found a piece of log and placed his pistol and blinker tube on it, then he waded in and pushed it ahead of him as he swam across the moonlit waters. Now and then he stopped swimming to watch and listen. He was within fifty feet of the shore when he saw the pathway through the trees. A squad of Japanese were walking along it heading toward the fallen log, or at least in that direction. There was no time for caution.

87

He kept his head low and swam slowly until his legs hit the soft bottom. He bellied into the brush and took his pistol and the blinker tube. He pushed his way toward the last place he had seen the chief, then paused in bewilderment. Everything seemed the same. He looked about, peering into the brush. He whistled softly, but there was no answer. He heard the alien voices of the Japanese echoing across the dark waters of the stream. They must be crossing the log.

" Chief! " said Bob in desperation.

" That you, Bob? " said Gary.

Bob leaped to one side. He saw Gary behind a tree. " Where's the chief? " he said.

"Behind me. Sick as a pup."

" Great! "

" Them the Aussies coming? " said Gary.

" Japs," said Bob.

Bob ran to Gary. He could see the chief still lying on the ground. Together they rolled him into the brush. Bob gripped Gary by the arm. " Stay with him! Keep him quiet! I've got to warn the others! "

Gary paled. " I wish I were going with you," he said.

Bob darted into the tangle, feeling vines and creepers rip at his clothing. He forced his way through to a clearing and looked back. There was nothing to be seen, but he knew the soldiers must be within fifty yards of him. It was too light for him to use the beach. He left the clearing and found a slightly easier way to get through the tangle, not twenty feet from the beach. Behind him he heard the faint sound of voices. They were reaching the beach, and he hoped it was on *this* side of Gary and Chief Daly.

The moonlight shone on the bay, lighting the rippling waters and the distant waters of the passage. Something seemed to move at the mouth of the bay and for a moment he thought it was *Grayfin* until he saw the tracery of masts and sails against the moonlight. It was a fishing schooner but that didn't mean it might not have Japanese aboard. They used every kind of water transport they could find. He wasn't sure if the schooner was heading into the bay or not.

He must be nearing the place where Krasnowski and his boys were hiding. He hoped they'd recognize him before they started shooting. One shot and the whole game would go down the chute. He paused to look back and as he did so he heard the humming of a motor in the sky. He looked up to see the moonlight flash on a plane's wings as it banked low over the bay. Icy fear swept through him. Maybe these weren't regular routine patrols. Maybe they knew something.

Bob ran forward and fell heavily over something. His hand touched the rough fabric of a rubber boat beneath a tangle of leaves and vines. " Kras? " he said breathlessly. There was no answer. His heart thudded against his ribs and his body was soaked in itching sweat. " Kras? " he said again. " Red? Slim? " Still no answer. Where had they gone? Maybe the Japs had found them, but that wasn't possible, for they hadn't reached that part of the beach as yet. *Unless some of them had come from the opposite direction!*

He crawled in between the two deflated boats and peered toward the southerly end of the bay. He saw nothing but the thick jungle and the white beach shining in the moonlight with the surf creaming up onto it and then withdrawing with a soft roaring sound. Where had they gone?

He looked back over his shoulder into the darkness of

the jungle, but there was nothing to be seen. Bob looked to his left along the beach and his heart skipped a beat or two. A file of men plodded slowly along the white sands, rifles at every angle, looking into the jungle or out into the bay. The moonlight was pouring into the area where the boats had been hidden. They should have carried them twenty yards farther into the tangle. There was no chance for Bob to run now. He lay flat and pulled his automatic from its holster. Seven rounds of .45 was hardly enough to stop those Japanese, and the racket would arouse every soldier and native for half a mile or more.

The schooner was moving slowly into the cove with flapping sails. The sails came drifting down and the faint beating of an auxiliary motor echoed over the water. The plane had banked again out over the passage and winged its way over the schooner. With all those activities it was hardly possible for the shore party to contact the commandos, if indeed they were in the bay area at all.

Bob closed his eyes to regain his strength and courage. Suddenly a vivid picture came to him of *Grayfin* slanting down to watery safety in the darkness of the depths, and he wished with all his heart he was within that stout hull.

The voices came closer. He opened his eyes. He lay between the two low humps of the deflated boats covered by their inadequate camouflage. There was nothing he could do but lie there and take whatever came. All he hoped was that the others had escaped and that his capture would warn them.

A command rang out. Bob opened his eyes. The squad had halted on the beach directly in line with the hidden boats. At the feet of the soldiers Bob could see the marks where the two boats had been hauled out of the surf. The shore party had wiped out the deeper marks, but not all of them. The men stood there talking. A match flared up to light a face intent on igniting a cigarette. One of them laughed. Other cigarettes flared up. They looked out into the clearly lighted bay to see the schooner moving in the direction of the hidden cove. That was all Gary needed, what with having a sick man on his hands, unable to move from their hiding place.

One of the men looked directly at Bob, as though something puzzled him, and Bob felt those dark eyes boring into his skull. For a moment the man stood there, unmoving. Bob did not dare blink an eye.

A command rang out. The Japanese marched off along the beach. Bob dropped his head and did not look up until the voices faded away. The schooner was entering the cove. He could hear her slowly running auxiliary engine.

Bob bellied back from beneath the boats and took cover in the denser growth. " Kras! " he called out. " Red! Slim! " There was no answer except the soft murmuring of the night wind through the tangle and the roaring of the surf on the beach.

8

IT took Bob more than an hour to work his way back toward the cove, keeping well back from the brightly lighted beach. The bay seemed deserted, but he knew those Japanese would work their way back on patrol to the shacks in the cove. He had no idea who had been on the second craft that had come into the cove. Once it had passed the point, he had not seen it or heard the sound of its auxiliary engine. There had been no more planes overhead.

The moon was at its zenith when he reached the stream. He found it easily enough by walking right into it. He paused to listen. He caught a faint glimpse of lamplight where the shacks were in the cove and one light farther out that was either on the wharf or on one of the boats moored there.

Gary must be sweating it out, wherever he was hiding with Chief Daly. If the chief had not recovered by now, it would be a problem to get him out to *Grayfin* when the submarine came in from the rendezvous before dawn of the next day. Commander Currie should not have listened to Daly and his desire for one more action against the enemy before he was returned to the States as an instructor. By letting Daly lead the shore landing party, the commander had endangered the lives of the other men, as well as those of the commandos. On the other hand, Daly had looked and acted like the very picture of health aboard the *Grayfin* and Commander Currie would never have allowed him to lead the shore party if he had had the slightest suspicion that the chief was not well. It was one of the breaks of the game, and war is never a game.

Bob faded back into the thick tangle and felt his way through to where he had left Gary and the chief. He remembered he had not agreed on some sign of recognition with Gary, but there was one they had used in the dangerous work of being coast watchers. Softly he whistled a few bars of "Chattanooga Choo-Choo," then waited tensely. Minutes drifted past. He heard a noise over at the buildings. He walked farther into the brush. Ten feet from a pathway or the beach and things began to get vague and mixed up and fifty feet from them a person could get thoroughly lost, for there were no landmarks, nothing to distinguish one's position.

He paused and looked about, then whistled softly. The answer came from behind him. He turned. " Gary? " he called.

" Who else? "

Bob crouched beside Gary. " How is he? " he asked.

Daly raised his head. " I'll live," he said. " It hit me suddenly." He winced in pain. " It's been years since I've had an attack like this."

" Can you walk? " asked Bob.

" Maybe a little," said the chief.

There was no use in recriminations. Bob dropped flat beside his two companions. " I went back to the boats," he said. " Krasnowski and the others are gone. No sign of 'em anywhere. That Jap patrol passed right by the boats with me lying in between them. For a moment I thought perhaps one of the Japs had seen me. They kept on going toward the other end of the bay."

" We heard another boat come into the cove," said Daly.

Bob nodded. " An auxiliary schooner. I couldn't see who was aboard."

" Fishermen, I guess," said Gary.

" Or more Jap soldiers," said the chief. His face contorted with pain.

" I'll go back and look for Kras and the others," said Bob.

" Maybe some other Japs got them," said Gary.

" There was no sign of a fight or anything. We didn't hear any shooting. I thought at first they were hiding near the rubber boats and I called out to them, but no one answered. Beats me where they went."

" It's getting late," said Daly. " You've got to locate those commandos before it gets too dark to find them."

" They were supposed to be around·here, weren't they? " asked Gary. " Bob has been all over the lot and hasn't seen hide or hair of 'em."

" It doesn't make any sense," said the chief.

" I'll bet we're twenty-four hours too early," said Gary.

No one spoke, but they were *thinking* plenty. The idea of trying to keep under cover during daylight the next day on into another moonlit night, with the bay area crawling with Japanese patrols, boats, and planes wasn't exactly calculated to have a pleasing effect.

" Maybe we ought to go back to *Grayfin* before dawn," said Gary, " and try it again at dusk tomorrow."

" You know how difficult it was to get in here and get ashore," said the chief fiercely. " We'd never get another break like that. No, we stay here until we find those Aussies! "

" Or the Japs find us," said Gary dryly.

94

The wind shifted a little and the faint sound of voices came from the area beyond the point. There seemed to be a lot of them.

The chief wiped the sweat from his taut face. " You lads go back down the beach and try to find Kras and the boys, and get a lead on the commandos. I'll lay low and try not to make a sound like a good little boy. Take the tommy gun, Lunt. The pistol will be enough for me."

The way he said it made Gary and Bob look closely at him. They knew what was in his mind. There were seven rounds in the heavy automatic; six for the Japanese and one for Chief Daly. It was his way. He seemed to know well enough that his chances of getting back to the *Grayfin* were practically nil.

Bob stood up. " We'll be back after dark," he said.

" We'll whistle ' Chattanooga Choo-Choo,' " added Gary.

The chief nodded. He looked up at them. " First things first," he said quietly. " Your job is to get those commandos off this island and into *Grayfin*. First and last, that's the job, *and don't you ever forget it.*"

Bob led the way through the jungle. They did not look back. Two hundreds yards from the chief's hiding place Gary stopped and looked back. " The old bullhead had to go along on this detail," he said. " Just to prove to us that he didn't earn his medals by re-upping after twenty years."

" Us? " said Bob. " Seems to me it was you who did all the talking."

" Well, he didn't have to jeopardize all of us just to prove it to me."

Bob turned. " Listen," he said, " Chief Daly was the best man for this job and you know it. It was a break and a bad one, but we can't get any results standing here crying about it."

Gary gripped Bob by the shoulder. " Sorry," he said.

" Come on then! Save that anger for the Japs. You'll need it, Mac."

Bob led the way back toward the hidden rubber boats. There was no sign of the three missing seamen. Gary scouted along the beach and came tearing back. " Japs! " he said. " A whole squad of them! Heading this way! "

This time Bob did not stay near the hidden boats. He led Gary well back into the tangle and they dropped down to peer beneath the growth toward the beach. Bob felt a lot better, in one way. With two pistols and Gary handling the submachine gun they would well take care of a squad of the enemy standing in the open, but the racket would arouse the whole bay area, and he didn't want that.

" Man! " whispered Gary. " How can they miss those boats? "

" If they spot them, we'd better hightail it out of here," Bob answered.

" I wasn't planning to stick around," said Gary.

The Japanese came even with the boats. The moonlight was more revealing than it had been before. They did not stop this time but kept tramping slowly back along the beach.

" I wonder how the chief will feel when he hears that mob," said Gary.

Bob peered in the direction from which the Japanese had come. Maybe Kras, Red, and Slim had gone that way. He hoped they hadn't gone back into the jungle and become lost. " Come on," he said. " We'll work along the edge of the jungle. We can make better time that way."

They drifted along the edge of the jungle, just out of

the welter of moonlight that shone on the white beach almost like daylight. The bay curved far to the left, eventually meeting the mouth of it that opened onto Sibutu Passage. There was no sign of life until they were halfway up the side of the bay opposite the cove and then Gary slapped Bob on the arm and dived into cover. They crawled back into the brush. Bob turned and looked back. He hadn't seen anything but he now heard a faint sound of voices. He narrowed his eyes. A tall man clad in dark clothing had appeared near a broken-backed fishing boat that lay half buried in the sand. " That's no Jap," he said over his shoulder to Gary.

Gary crawled up beside Bob. " Nope, unless he's got the good old Jap name of Krasnowski."

Bob crawled toward the beach. " Kras! " he called out.

The tall seaman dropped behind the wrecked boat and thrust the heavy automatic rifle over the edge of it. " That you, Bob? " he called out.

" Me and Gary," said Bob inelegantly.

" Where you been? "

" Get out of that moonlight! " said Gary. " You loco or something? The place is crawling with Nips."

The tall seaman came into the brush and dropped beside them, wiping the sweat from his face. " Man, oh man," he said, " It's been a rough night. Where's the chief? "

" We'll tell you later," said Bob. " Where did you go? Where are Red and Slim? "

" We were hiding out near the boats after you left when Slim suddenly says he thinks you went the wrong way. We argued over whether we were supposed to look for the commandos to the north or south of the bay. I said it was north, like the chief said, Slim says it was south, and Kelly was in the middle. We figured there wasn't much

97

time, so we took a chance and came this way. I stayed near the beach to watch out for Japs and to see if you guys would show up. Later on I saw those Japs. I had to get off the beach, so I got back into a swamp and had a rough time finding my way out. Red and Slim had found a pathway and wanted to see where it went. I stayed behind to cover the beach with the BAR."

"Where are they now?"

Krasnowski shrugged. "Somewhere back in there. Where's the chief?"

Bob told the story of Daly's sickness to the tall seaman. "He's hiding out back there," he said.

"Great!" said Krasnowski. "Right where those crazy Japs are! That's all we need! What do we do now?"

"You're next in command," said Gary.

Krasnowski began to scrape the mud of the swamp from his legs. "If we don't find those commandos before *Grayfin* makes the rendezvous, we're stuck here for another day. What'd Daly say?"

"I'll quote," said Gary dryly. "First things first. Your job is to get those commandos off this island and into *Grayfin*. First and last, that's the job, *and don't you ever forget it.*"

Krasnowski wrinkled his brow. "You mean . . . ?"

"Exactly," said Gary.

"I'm not about to leave him here, no matter what he says," said the seaman.

Bob stood up. "Well, in that case, we'd better find Red and Slim and see if we can find those commandos. Time's awastin'!"

Krasnowski led the way along the edge of the beach. Far across the bay they could see the faint lights in the cove. Somewhere near those lights lay Chief Daly, sick and helpless, with a Japanese patrol close by. They might stumble over him in the darkness of the jungle, or something might give him away, perhaps an unstifled cry or groan. Maybe he would get delirious and give himself away.

"This way," said Krasnowski.

Bob looked up the uninviting pathway. It was wider than the one he had stumbled upon on the other side of the bay — wide enough for cars or trucks, perhaps even some of the small tanks the enemy favored in these areas. The overhanging branches had thatched themselves over the pathway forming a tunnel of darkness and danger.

"We'd better go in at intervals," said Bob. "Say fifty feet apart. That way some of us might be able to make a break if we're trapped." He looked back at Krasnowski. "I think I can outrun you and I'm not carrying a BAR. I'll go first."

"Take your time, kid," said Krasnowski. "Don't worry. I've got twenty rounds of .30/06 in here that says you *won't* get trapped."

Bob walked softly into the pathway. The ground was damp and covered with leaves, so he didn't make much noise. The wind worked its way through the surrounding tangle, moving the brush, rubbing branches one against another. It wasn't quite the place Bob would have chosen for a quiet evening walk. He drew his pistol from its holster and carried it in his hand as he walked on. The sweetish, cloying odor of rotting vegetation filled the jungle. Birds twittered in the dimness. Now and then he reached an area where faint shafts of moonlight came down through the overhead tangle and in a clearing he found several footprints. Whoever had made them had not been wearing the Japanese *tabi*, footwear with the large toe

99

separated from the rest of the toes.

Something splashed in the swamp. Something scuttled swiftly across the pathway behind him. His nerves were getting honed to a fine edge. Then suddenly it grew lighter as the vegetation thinned out and he rounded a curve in the pathway and stopped short. A man stood with his back toward Bob, looking toward a place where a stream crossed a wide, moonlit clearing. Bob whistled softly, then jumped to one side.

The man turned, swinging up a pistol, thumbing down the safety catch. It was Red Kelly. He shook his head as he recognized Bob. " Man, you gave me a start! " he said.

" Kras and Gary are behind me. Where's Slim? "

Red shrugged. " We ran into a native who could speak a little English. He agreed to guide Slim farther up this pathway."

" For what? "

Red tilted his head to one side. " For *what?* The gook said he had seen some white men inland day before yesterday."

" The commandos? "

" Who knows? Slim took a chance. Where's the chief? "

Once again Bob had to explain what had happened to Daly. " He's hiding back there within spitting distance of the Jap camp," he added.

Red rubbed his jaw. " Maybe one of us ought to go back there and take care of him," he said. " I'll go."

Krasnowski came up the path carrying the heavy automatic rifle. " Nobody goes back," he said. " I'm taking charge now. One man couldn't do anything for the chief. First we find the commandos, then we try to help the chief."

" That's not the way I see it," said Red coldly.

"It's the way *I* see it," said the big seaman.

Bob nodded. "It's the way the chief wanted it."

Krasnowski looked at Bob. "You make a pretty good scout, kid. You want to keep on?"

Bob nodded. He crossed the clearing. The pathway was wider and more open here, ascending a slight slope up out of the swampy area, and once when he looked back he could see through an opening in the treetops all the way down to the bay. The moon was waning. Far to his right, and almost indistinguishable, he thought he saw the lights of the Japanese camp.

The moon was dying when he came to an open field. On the far side of the field were some thatched huts, but none of them looked as though they were occupied, or had been for a long time. Bob held up his left arm to halt the others. Krasnowski padded forward. "What do you think, Bob?" he asked.

"Slim is somewhere up ahead," said Bob. "I'll work toward those huts, staying around the side of the field under cover of the trees." He trotted forward, angling toward the side of the field. There was no sign of life about the huts. Bob bellied close to one of them. It was quiet, except for the sighing of the tropic wind through the trees. He was about to turn back when he caught the faint odor of something. He raised his head. Once again he caught it. Burning tobacco!

Bob rested his chin on his crossed forearms. Japanese smoked tobacco and so did the natives. He looked up at the sky. The moon was very low, giving just about enough time for them to get back to the rubber boats. They'd never be able to work their way to the boats without moonlight. They had to start at once.

Bob got up and crouched. He walked between two of

101

the huts. The tobacco smell grew stronger. He peered around a hut. An arm shot about his neck, drawing back hard. Something hard and dirty — a strong hand — closed about his open mouth. " Quiet, Yank," came an unmistakable Aussie voice. " You want to wake up the whole island? "

Bob shook his head. The Australian released him. Bob turned to see an incredibly emaciated man, taller by half a head than Bob, dressed in ragged, filthy garments. An Aussie hat, left side of the brim turned up, hung at the back of the Australian's dark hair. " Howdy, cobber," said Bob. " We've come to take you home."

The Australian nodded. " So your cobber said. One of my mates went to get the rest of the lads. They should be here any minute. We were down at the beach at the right time and never saw hide or hair of you. When the Jap patrol came this way we drifted back in here, figuring you'd be back."

A faint birdcall came through the darkness of the jungle. The Australian threw back his head, cupped his dirty hands about his mouth, and imitated the call perfectly. " That'll be the lads," he said.

Slim Polk grinned at Bob from where he stood behind a tree. " Man," he said in appreciation, " you should have seen the look on your pan when Bert grabbed you."

Four men came out of the tangle. One of them smiled at Bob and Slim. " Thank God," he said. " The thought of having to stay on this blasted island another night was almost too much for me. I'm Lieutenant Keene, Scots Guards, on commando duty with my Australian friends."

" There were supposed to be six men picked up, sir," said Bob.

The commandos glanced at each other out of the corners of their eyes. Keene looked away from Bob. "Jack Hogan didn't make it," he said quietly.

"We'd better get moving," said Bob. "We've just about time to get back to the boats. We'll hole up until before dawn. The submarine is due in then. With luck, we'll be out of Sibutu Passage by broad daylight."

Bob led the way back to Krasnowski, Red, and Gary. There was no conversation among the ten hurrying men as they worked their way down the pathway. There was just about enough time to make it to the boats.

The moon was almost gone when Gary and Bob crawled through the thick brush to where they could see the faint, humped outlines of the boats. Bob breathed a sigh of relief. He bellied forward. It was very quiet except for the sighing of the wind and the rushing of the surf. He crawled between the boats and looked toward the beach. There was no sign of life. He turned to crawl back and his eyes fell upon something. The vines and creepers that had concealed the side of one of the boats had fallen aside. A two-foot gash had been sliced clean through the thick, rubberized canvas of the boat. He stared at it unbelievingly. He looked at the other boat. It was gashed even worse than the first. A horrible thought came to him. He raised his head and looked over one of the boats. The brush seemed to blossom red and orange flowers and the sharp, staccato chattering of a light machine broke the stillness.

Bob jumped to his feet and ran at a crouch toward the jungle as slugs slapped the trees beside him and tore at the dirt. Another gun opened fire, the chattering reports echoing and reechoing across the darkening bay. A hand grabbed Bob by the shirt and dragged him into the brush. He was pushed ahead. He saw the back of an Australian

103

ahead of him, and the man was running through the dark jungle, standing not upon the order of his going.

A branch slapped alongside Bob's head. His eyes filled with sudden tears. He stumbled and went down on one knee, but a hand dragged him to his feet. The racing fugitives splashed into knee-deep water, showering it back on both sides as they forced their way through the dark swamp. Slugs still tore through the tangle, slapping into trees or whining eerily overhead.

They ran until they could run no farther, then fell prone on a marshy hummock, weapons thrust to point back the way from which they had come. The shooting had died away.

" By the Lord Harry! " said Lieutenant Keene between gulps of air. " Ambushed within a few hours of getting off this accursed island."

It became quiet except for the harsh breathing of the exhausted men and the moaning of the wind through the jungle. The moon was fully gone. Somewhere, out there in the darkness, *Grayfin* was waiting for the rendezvous that would never be made.

9

A HAND shook Bob awake. He opened his eyes to see faint gray light filtering down from the treetops. If *Grayfin* had come into the rendezvous to wait vainly for a signal from Bob, she was long gone now, to return in darkness. What Bob and the others had feared had come true. The worst of it was that the boats were useless and that the Japanese knew they were on the island.

Lieutenant Keene slapped at a buzzing insect. "Doesn't take them long to learn you're here," he said.

They all sat around the officer, damp and shivering. In the growing light Bob could see the thin, drawn faces of the commandos. *They had been hiding out on the island for over two years.* There was another thing he noticed. Their weapons were bright and clean.

"Council of war," said the officer. "We know the submarine is no longer waiting out there for us. It will not return for about another twenty-four hours."

"We've got to get out to her," said Tim Harkness, one of the Australians. "With no boats we're in a bind."

"We can't go out to her until before the next dawn," said Krasnowski. He rubbed a bit of mud from the barrel of his automatic rifle.

"We've got to get out of this blasted swamp and into a hideout," said Bert Campbell.

Red Kelly squeezed an insect bite. "Don't forget about Chief Daly," he said. He looked accusingly at big Krasnowski as though it was the seaman's personal fault.

"Any suggestions, mates?" said the officer.

Gary looked up. "One or two of us can swim out there after dark and try to find her," he said.

"Too risky," said Slim Polk.

Bob nodded his head in agreement. "The Japs have two boats in the cove at the north end of the bay," he said. "A motor sampan and an auxiliary schooner."

"He forgot something," said Gary. "There are Japs all over the place."

The officer thoughtfully rubbed his jaw. "Looking for *us*," he said. "Maybe they're so busy looking for us they haven't time to guard their boats."

Bert Campbell grinned. "I'm beginning to get the idea," he said.

Bob leaned forward. "Maybe if a few of us kept the Japs busy, the rest of you could move in quietly and take over those boats."

Keene glanced at him. "You should have been a commando, Yank," he said with an easy smile.

"Listen!" said Gary.

They all raised their heads. Somewhere over the jungle sounded the humming of a plane, with that peculiar intermittent sound of a Japanese motor.

"Don't look up," said Krasnowski.

"Our faces are so dirty they'd never be able to spot them in this pesthole," Tim Harkness said.

Keene stood up. "It'll take us a good part of the day to work through this swamp and circle around to come in behind that cove. Bob, do you know the lay of the land well enough there?"

"Not too well, but I think I can guide you in."

The officer nodded. He looked down at his small command. "You might as well know right now that if any of you are badly wounded, or incapacitated in any way, the rest of us must go on without you."

The plane came low over the treetops until the roaring of its engine drowned out the voice of the officer.

Lieutenant Keene checked his heavy Webley pistol, then thrust it back into its holster. "You Americans can let yourselves be taken prisoner if you like. The information the rest of us have has taken us two years to accumulate and all of it has been committed to memory by each one of us. The Japanese must not discover that we have this information." He paused for a moment. "We have agreed among ourselves, therefore, that none of us can be taken alive. We have also agreed that if one of us is helpless, or unable in any way to take his own life before the Japs reach him, the duty will be taken over by another one of us. We do not ask you Americans to take your own lives in preference to being captured, but we do ask you to finish off any one of us if you are the only possible means of so doing. Is that clear?"

Mud squelched under soaked shoes and boots as the men all stood up. The commandos looked at the five Americans. One by one the men of the shore landing party nodded their heads.

Lieutenant Keene stepped off into the dark, knee-deep water. "Come on, lads," he said cheerfully. "It's a nice day for a bit of a wade."

Bob slung his blinker tube over his shoulder. He did not look at the others as he followed the officer. Two things filled his mind. The thought of having to kill one of these courageous commandos, and the thought of Chief Daly,

107

sick and helpless, lying so close to the enemy camp.

Now and then a plane would pass over the swamp, sometimes so low that the struggling men could see the flashing of the sun from it. As the sun rose higher and higher, so did the heat and humidity of the swamp. Noisome, fetid odors haunted the swamp. Great, lazy butterflies of exquisite colorations and patterns drifted through the sunlit patches. Insects buzzed, hummed, rasped, chirped, and creaked, mingling their noise with the sounds of many birds who darted among the trees. Every so often something heavy would splash in the dark waters. Crawling things draped themselves over fallen logs, or clung to thick vines, eyeing the mud-plastered, sweating intruders with bright and unblinking eyes.

There was water everywhere, but none of it to drink. They could not take chances with it. Such swamps were the lairs of malaria, yellow fever, dengue fever, jungle fever, and many other tropical sicknesses and diseases. It was sheer hell to splash along, sometimes chest-deep in the water and not be able to drink it.

There was no time to rest, for it was a long way around to the cove, and the going was agonizingly slow. Bob was amazed at the stamina and fiber of the commandos, all of whom looked as though a strong wind might break them in two, so thin were they from fever, lack of food, and too much exertion. They had been running and hiding for over two years, and now they were at it again, with the end so close in sight, but not yet achieved, and perhaps it never would be achieved.

They reached the edge of the stinking morass sometime in the middle of the afternoon and most of them dropped to rest, but there must always be guards. The Japanese were excellent jungle fighters, as they proved all the way from Malaya to New Guinea. If one of those slowly circling planes had spotted the fugitives in the swamp, there might be a reception party waiting for them on the higher ground, as there had been one back at the ruined rubber boats. The enemy knew well enough that whoever had hidden those boats there was still on the island. It was only a matter of time before they would be killed or captured.

The sun was slanting to the west when Bob stepped out onto the narrow pathway that followed the southern bank of the dark, meandering stream that flowed into the cove. It was difficult to tell how far away they were from the cove.

Lieutenant Keene wiped the sweat from his insect-swollen face. " Is this it? " he asked huskily.

" Yes. I'm quite sure."

" How far is the cove? "

" Perhaps a mile. Perhaps more."

Keene nodded. " Where is this petty officer of yours hidden, Bob? "

" Somewhere down there, within shouting distance of the Jap camp."

" Pray God we can find him," said the officer.

The men filed out onto the damp pathway, breathing hard, dripping sweat, scratching, and rubbing at bites and stings. Five American naval seamen, an officer of the Scots Guards, and four lean Australians. Every man checked his weapons. All the commandos were armed with Webley pistols and Harry Armitage, Tad Jones, and Lieutenant Keene carried submachine guns. The officer held up his tommy gun. " Each of us has but one drum of ammunition for these tommy guns," he said. " We haven't had a parachute drop in three months."

Gary looked at his tommy gun. "One drum for this," he said.

Krasnowski patted his web harness. "Twenty rounds in the BAR," he said, "and two extra clips. Sixty rounds all told."

"Not much ammo with which to start a war," said the officer, "but we'll do the best we can, eh, chaps?" He slapped Bob on the shoulder. "Let's go!"

It was getting darker by the minute in the green tunnel of the pathway. Bob kept fifty feet ahead of the officer, ready at a second's notice to leap into the brush to clear the way for the automatic weapons behind him if he should run into a party of Japanese.

The sun was suddenly gone, leaving a pale grayness in the jungle, but splashing the sky with a brilliance of hues in gold, red, yellow, and orange, blended with faint pink.

Bob stopped and the officer came up behind him. "Tell the rest of them to come up here while we can still see," said Bob, "and I'll show the lay of the land as best I can."

They gathered around him in the dying light as he traced out a crude map on the damp earth, until each man understood it.

Keene took Gary by the arm. "You know where Chief Daly is," he said. "Bert Campbell will go with you. Tim, Harry, and Tad will make the diversion beyond the cove. I told you lads what to do. Red and Slim will cover this pathway. Tad, you let Red have your tommy gun. We'll have to parcel out our heavy artillery. Krasnowski and Bob will work with me. I need Bob to guide us to those buildings in the dark. It's our job to get one of those boats. Understood?"

No one spoke, but every head nodded.

"The whole success of the plan lies in each party lying

low and out of sight until the time for the attack. There will be Jap patrols. We have to time this attack to almost a split second. The submarine will be lying out in the bay in the darkness before the dawn. If we're too early, we'll alert every Jap on this bay and we won't have a chance of getting out to the submarine. If we're too late, we'll be stuck with a boat and no submarine and I don't have to tell you what our chances of getting out of this bay and into Sibutu Passage will be. We'll be hunted down like mad dogs. The signal for the attack will be the diversion created by Tim, Harry, and Tad to draw off the Japs at the cove into their fire. Red and Slim will keep station near this path to stop any reinforcements from inland. If no reinforcements show up, then you two lads will join us at the cove. We'll more than likely need you. Bert and Gary will cover the southern approach to the cove. Is everything clear?"

Every head nodded again.

"Start out then, and God be with all of you."

Gary and Bert vanished into the thick tangle alongside the trail. Tad and his two mates waded into the stream and crossed it to vanish into the jungle on the far side. Red and Slim stepped off the trail into the jungle. For a moment the sound of their passage came faintly to those still on the trail and then it was gone.

"That leaves us," said the officer to his two companions.

Bob smiled weakly. Krasnowski checked his BAR. "All set, sir," he said. He handed the two extra ammunition clips to Bob.

Bob led off down the darkened pathway until he reached the fallen log. He crossed it quickly, followed by the others. He led them into the jungle alongside the trail until he could see the dim outline of the rusted corrugated shack. There was no sign of life around it. Quickly Bob crossed the wider trail that led from the camp and worked his way into the tangle on the point that thrust itself out into the dark waters of the bay.

It was all very quiet except for the sighing of the wind through the trees and the dull sound of the surf. Bob went down flat and worked his way to the vantage point he had found the first time he had been there. Keene and Krasnowski crawled up beside him. A dim light showed in the schooner cabin. The sampan was dark and seemingly deserted. Two of the buildings had lights in them.

" What time does the patrol go out? " asked Keene.

" After the rise of the moon."

" When do they come back? "

" While it is still moonlight."

" Does another patrol go out after that? "

" I don't know. I suppose so."

Keene bit his lip. " I'd like to hit them when they are short of men. Can't be helped. We have to hit them right on time or the whole business will blow up in our faces. I'll take first guard. You two lads get some sleep."

" I can't sleep, sir," said Bob.

The officer handed Bob the tommy gun. " Then Kras and I will take a crack at it. If anything suspicious or unusual happens, wake me up."

Bob lay quietly, holding the submachine gun in his hands. He was tired, hungry, thirsty, and filthy. Right on those boats and in the shacks there would be food and water. The only thing was that the enemy thought they had a prior right to the food and the water, and the boats, for that matter.

He looked out onto the bay. The last vestiges of light were gone. He thought he saw a faint blue light out there,

112

but it quickly faded away. Maybe the *Grayfin* had surfaced and was looking for her shore party. It wasn't likely. Commander Currie could not risk his boat and his crew no matter how worried he was about his missing men.

Faintly, ever so faintly, came the soft, dull beating of an engine out in the bay, or perhaps beyond it in Sibutu Passage. It seemed to be echoed by the sound of a plane engine winging over the island. The enemy was alert, all right.

Darkness filled the area except for the faint light on the schooner and the lights in the shacks. The wind shifted a little. Something splashed in the cove. Someone was singing over at the shacks. Probably a soldier lonely for his home, or perhaps a radio bringing music from Tokyo.

Time drifted past until Bob was aware of the faint light of the rising moon. Slowly it grew until the moonlight drifted down into the cove and sparkled on the dark water. Voices sounded from the shacks. There was a rattling of equipment and a sharp command or two. He could make out the line of men standing there; then at a command they started off toward the pathway that led across the foot of the point and on toward the beach. He watched them tramp past, talking and laughing a little. They seemed so sure of themselves and yet they must know someone had come ashore in those rubber boats. There must be many more Japanese out, perhaps surrounding the swamp. There must be boat patrols in the bay. They were evidently quite sure no one could get out of the net they had woven.

His eyes grew heavy with sleep after the patrol had long since vanished down the moonlit beach. He touched Krasnowski. The seaman awoke and nodded. He crawled to the edge of the brush and thrust the heavy automatic

113

rifle across a fallen tree. Bob lay down and closed his eyes. He drifted off into sleep.

The hard hand closed over Bob's mouth and another hand shook him awake. "Pardon the dirty hand," said the officer, "but I didn't want you to cry out."

Bob sat up. It was dark again, with a clinging, mysterious darkness that seemed to move back and forth. "Is it time?" he whispered hoarsely.

Keene looked at his watch. "Almost," he said.

Bob rubbed his eyes. It was warm in among the trees, but even so, a coldness settled within him. Somewhere he had once read that the hour or so before the dawn is when a man's spirits and morale are at their lowest ebb. He knew now that it was true.

Krasnowski eased his knife in its sheath. He placed the heavy rifle across his lap and looked at Bob. "If anything happens to me," he said quietly, "you can take over this BAR. Can you handle one?"

"I qualified on it," said Bob.

It was very quiet. There were no lights around the cove. The water lapped softly on the beach. The wind moaned through the trees.

"The patrol came back just before the moon died," said the big seaman. "Another one went out, but they went back into the bush. I hope they didn't run into Red and Slim."

"There wasn't any shooting," said the officer. "Of course, that doesn't mean anything either, if you're surprised."

Bob checked his blinker tube, cupping his hands about the mouth of the tube. It was working fine.

Keene looked at his watch again. "I'll go in first," he said. "Kras, you stay a few paces behind me and to one side. Bob, you back up Kras. If I get hit badly, you know what to do."

They both nodded. They knew what to do, all right.

Keene checked his watch again. " Almost time," he said. He led the way to the pathway and stepped out upon it, swinging forward his tommy gun. Kras looked at Bob and smiled faintly.

Keene pulled down his wide-brimmed hat. " Now," he said.

A gun cracked from beyond the camp of the Japanese. Another spoke. A man yelled. An automatic weapon stuttered briefly, died away, crackled again.

" Come on," said Lieutenant Keene. He ran softly down the pathway toward the shacks.

10

A SHADOWY cluster of men ran from the shacks into the thick, echoing darkness north of the cove. Gunfire flamed. A rataplan of echoes slammed back and forth across the wide clearing, and then the Japanese vanished into the woods.

" Get to the boats," said Keene over his shoulder.

The jungle sparkled with gunflashes. A man screamed and suddenly it was cut off. Smoke drifted back across the clearing. A door banged open revealing a rectangle of yellow light, Lieutenant Keene raced toward the door. The light was partially blocked by a man. The tommy gun stuttered and the man was literally blown back into the room by the impact of the heavy slugs. The Englishman leaped into the room, spraying fire from one side to the other. Glass shattered and the light went out.

" Come on," said Krasnowski, running toward the sagging wharf. Two men tumbled over the side of the schooner and ran toward the two Americans, shouting in Japanese. Krasnowski touched the trigger of the BAR. The two Japanese went back into the water.

A Japanese clambered out of the sampan, screaming and waving his arms. Bob swung sideways and fired once. The man fell heavily onto the deck of the boat, then rolled sideways to fall over the far side into the water.

Bob looked over his shoulder. The gunfire was heavier. A grenade exploded in the tangle of jungle.

Krasnowski stopped beside the schooner. Three men ran along the deck toward him. He emptied the BAR into them. The empty shell cases tinkled on the wharf and bounced into the water. Bob stepped up alongside Krasnowski as the seaman took the empty magazine from the weapon. Bob shoved a refill magazine into the smoking weapon.

Keene stepped into the edge of the jungle to meet a clump of yelling Japanese. He emptied his tommy gun into them and darted behind a shack as a grenade exploded in the clearing, the sharp flash of light illuminating the area. In that instant Bob saw that every Japanese was down on the ground.

Krasnowski kicked open a scuttle slide. He jumped to one side and waited. A gun flashed in the darkness below the scuttle. Bob fired twice down into the darkness. Something fell heavily.

There was a savage burst of gunfire in the jungle and then it grew quiet. Bob looked at Krasnowski. The big sea-man wiped the sweat from his face. " Suddenly I feel awfully lonely," he said.

" You chaps all right? " called out Keene.

" The boats are empty," said Bob.

" Are you sure? You must be sure! " said the officer.

" Bob! Kras! Lieutenant Keene! " called out Red Kelly, raising his voice.

" Over here! " called out Keene.

The two seamen came out of the darkness. " Is it all right, sir? " asked Slim.

" It's awfully quiet," said Red.

Tim Harkness came trotting through the darkness. Tad

Jones limped along behind him. " All clear over here," said the tall Australian.

" Where's Harry? " said the officer.

" He won't be coming along," said Tad.

Bob stared at the noncommittal commando, until he realized that these men were used to living with violence and sudden death, and that their composure was only a cover-up for how they really felt.

Someone whistled sharply from the far side of the stream.

" That will be Bert and the Yanks," said the officer.

Bert and Gary came walking slowly to the edge of the clearing with Chief Daly between them, his arms across their shoulders. The chief grinned weakly. " I missed all the fun," he said.

" Take a look at the boats with Kras and Bob," said the officer to Tim and Tad.

The two Australians ran forward. Tim drew out his pistol. " All right, cobber," he said to Tad. He dropped down the scuttle while Tad stood to one side with his tommy gun ready. There was a sharp outcry and the cracking of a pistol, loud in the confined space. Tim clambered out on deck, wiping a bright streak of blood from his tanned face. " Devil had a knife," he said. " Spoiled me handsome phiz," he added. He looked at the officer. " That's the last of the lot, sir."

The fire in the shack gathered strength. The crackling of the flames sounded louder and smoke drifted across the clearing.

" Check for food, water, grenades, or anything else we can use," said Lieutenant Keene. He looked at Chief Daly. " Are you all right? "

Daly nodded. " I can steer a course, sir."

"Which boat should we take? The sampan?"

Daly shook his head. "The schooner. You've got sails when you run out of fuel. We might have a long way to go if we don't find *Grayfin*."

"Right! Let's scuttle the sampan."

Red Kelly walked to the boat and went down below. In a few minutes he came up on deck. "Hand me that sledgehammer, Slim," he said. He took the heavy tool and vanished below again. Metal rang against metal as he smashed the engine and other machinery.

The little party gathered on the pier carrying things they might need. Two of the commandos rolled extra fuel drums onto the schooner's deck. Bob lashed them fast.

"Douse that fire in the shack," said Keene.

They threw water and dirt on the fire and it winked out, leaving a heavy pall of stinking smoke. The group gathered on the wharf as the sampan settled deeper and deeper into the water until the deck was awash.

"What time is the rendezvous?" asked the officer.

Bob looked at his watch. "We have about fifteen minutes, sir," he said. "I'll walk out on the point. They'll be able to see me there."

"Get cracking then."

Bob motioned to Gary, and the two of them walked from the pier through the smoky darkness to the path. Gary looked back. "I've never seen such efficiency," he said.

"They're professionals," said Bob. "I can see now how they've managed to survive this long."

They worked their way through the brush and trees to the narrow strip of beach at the tip of the small point. Now and then they heard faint noises as the rest of the group made ready the schooner.

119

Bob looked at his watch. " All right," he said.

" I hope no Jap is watching us," said Gary.

" We'll take a chance on that," said Bob as he raised the blinker tube. " All I know is I can't wait to leave this island paradise."

The wind shifted again and the surf rolled up almost to their feet, breaking on the beach. The bay was dark. Bob triggered out the recognition signal, waited two minutes, triggered it again, then repeated it a third time.

They stared into the windy darkness, but nothing showed. Not a quick flashing of light. Nothing.

Bob bit his lip. " Maybe they're looking for the signal from where we left the boats," he said. " That's more than half a mile from here."

" *Grayfin* has good lookouts," said Gary. " They'd be scanning the whole bay looking for trouble."

Bob nodded. Gary was right. They'd have to see the signal. He waited a few more minutes, then sent the signal three times with two-minute intervals.

Minutes dragged past. It was very quiet in the cove. They too were looking out into the bay for that faint blue winking light.

" What now? " Gary asked in a low voice. " They *have* to be out there! "

Bob leaned against a tree. There was a green sickness in the pit of his stomach. The sudden action and the swift, efficient killing had almost been too much for him. *They had to get off the island!*

" Once more," said Gary.

Bob's heart wasn't in it. He raised the tube and sent the signal for the third time. He stared into the darkness until his eyes began to play tricks on him.

Gary raised his head and looked up into the darkness.

120

"Listen!" he said tensely.

The faint, intermittent humming of an engine came to them. An almost indistinguishable blue light flicked up there. It was blue, all right, but it certainly wasn't a recognition signal.

"It's about a thousand feet too high," said Gary.

Bob knew what he meant. He looked out across the darkness of the bay, hoping to see the signal. The long tube of the blinker would shield the light from being seen from the sky.

A burst of sheer white light broke in the sky directly above the bay. A parachute flare swung uneasily in the wind as it drifted slowly toward the shore. The bay was empty of life. No familiar black conning tower and low-lying hull could be seen. If they had come in for the rendezvous, they would have stayed on the surface. It was impossible to submerge in those shallows. The *Grayfin* wasn't there because it had never come there, and it wouldn't come there now.

The flare flickered out over the island, plunging everything into blackness. Bob stood there with the blinker tube in his hand. The dawn would break before too long. If they meant to do anything, they had better do it at once.

"Bob?" said Gary.

"Yes?"

"No use in trying again, hey?"

Bob rubbed his free hand over Gary's short-cropped hair. "No use," he said tonelessly.

"We're wasting time here then."

Bob nodded. He looked out on the bay once more. He shook his head and followed Gary through the darkness to the clearing. Gary whistled the recognition signal and they walked out onto the wharf.

"No go, eh, Bob?" asked Daly.

"Nothing, Chief."

"I figured as much."

Lieutenant Keene walked up to them. "There's only one thing left to do," he said. "This place will be alive with Japs in a matter of an hour or so. We can go back into the bush and hide out or we can make a try by sea. What do you chaps think?"

"I'll never make it on land," said Daly.

"I'll take my chances at sea," said Krasnowski.

Keene nodded. "Who'll take the helm?"

Bob looked up. "I will. I have a lot of small boat experience. I'll need a man forward to conn. Gary here has eyes like a cat."

"The rest of us will get below or hide on deck," said the officer. "Do they have patrol boats in the bay?"

"Yes, sir," said Gary.

The officer hesitated. "My lads and I don't intend to surrender," he said quietly.

"We won't let you," said Daly. "Polk! Get below on that engine! Lieutenant Keene, you stay on deck with me! The rest of you get below after we cast off!"

"Chiefie sounds like his old self," said Gary to Bob.

"Get forward!" snapped Daly to Gary.

Bob took the rusty wheel in his hands. The engine kicked over, spluttered, and died. Once again it kicked over and then died away. Bob could hear Slim talking to it, cajoling it, cussing it. It spat into life again, rumbled erratically, then settled down into an asthmatic thudding sort of a sound.

"Cast off forward!" said Daly.

The line was drawn inboard and thrown on the dirty deck. "All clear forward," said Red Kelly.

" Cast off aft! " said the chief.

The after line was removed from the mooring post and drawn onto the deck. The little schooner drifted away from the wharf. The engine was put into gear at Bob's quiet command and the schooner headed out of the cove. She bobbed a little as she met the incoming surf, then surged into the water of the bay. Bob looked up at the sky. He couldn't see any exhaust flames, but neither could he hear the plane's motor above the thudding of the ancient auxiliary engine.

The men who were not needed went below into the noisome cabin of the schooner. A strong aura hung about the ancient craft — the mingled odors of fish, mildew, unpumped bilges, greasy food, and burnt gasoline.

They cleared the cove and putted out into the bay, rising and falling gently. Bob looked back toward the dark mouth of the cove. There was no sign of life there except a faint reddish eye of fire now and then from the ashes of the shack, like rubies on black velvet. Somewhere back there lay the lean, smiling Australian named Harry Armitage. Bob had spoken to him only a few times. Now he lay staring up at the dark sky with eyes that did not see.

" Port a little," said Gary.

Bob turned the wheel. A drifting log bumped alongside the unpainted hull of the schooner.

" Shall we try the blinker? " said the officer.

" No use," said Daly.

There was a long silence from the officer. " Then we try for the passage? "

" Yes, sir," said Daly. He winced in pain and gripped his abdomen.

" Is it bad, Chief? " Bob asked.

" I'll be all right," said the chief. " Watch that helm!

You're steering like a Marine!"

Bob grinned in the darkness. Daly would always be Daly. It was the one sure thing in the unsure world they were now living in.

They were halfway up the bay when Gary came running aft. "I saw a light out there," he said.

"*Grayfin?*" asked Bob eagerly.

"Cut the engine," said Daly.

The engine spluttered out into the silence. The schooner drifted with the wind and tide, the water lapping noisily alongside. Faintly came the sound of an engine across the dark waters.

"Submarine?" asked Keene.

Daly stood up and peered into the darkness. "No," he said at last. "Skipper would never bring her in here on the diesels. That's a gas engine."

"Patrol boat?"

Daly shrugged. "That or a fishing boat," he said. "Supposing they take a look-see at us?"

Keene patted his tommy gun. He stood up. "I suggest Bob change some of his clothing," he said, "so as to look like a native or a Jap as much as possible."

"Maybe I'd better stay in uniform," said Bob, a little nervously.

Keene looked sideways at him. "You think that makes a difference to *them*, lad?" he said softly.

Bob felt an icy coldness come over him.

"I'll round up some clothing," said the officer. He smiled in the darkness. "By the way, I speak excellent Japanese and the local native tongue. All my men speak the native tongue fluently. I hope we don't have to use it, as we did on the island, but it might get us by." He went below.

"Handy fellows," said Gary.

"Get forward!" snapped Daly.

Gary got.

Later Bob and Gary changed into some of the rather smelly, greasy clothing Keene brought up for them. The officer had changed also. "If the three of us can fool them," he said, "we might have a chance. If not, we have other means to convince them." He didn't have to elucidate. His meaning was clear enough.

"Mouth of the bay dead ahead!" called back Gary. "Two hundred yards!"

Bob swallowed hard. The smell of the Japanese clothing made him a little sick, or was it something else?

"We'll make it yet," said Keene.

Something broke into flaring white light above the bay. The parachute flare hung swaying in the dawn wind. The plane could be seen flying toward Sibutu Passage, but the flare hung over the bay. Two hundred yards away another boat swayed in the chop that was coming in from the passage. Half a dozen men stared keenly at the schooner. A small deck gun was mounted on the other boat, larger by half than the schooner.

"Act natural," said Keene.

Bob gripped the rusty wheel tightly and looked straight ahead. The flare was swinging down over the beach, although there was still plenty of light over the bay. Bob did not dare look at the other boat, but one thing had etched itself into his mind. She was carrying far too much radio antenna for a simple fishing boat and it wasn't likely the Japanese were passing out deck guns to native fishermen.

The schooner plunged deeply as she met the first of the big incoming waves of the bay mouth. A spray of water flew up over the bows and doused Gary, but he never turned a hair.

Any second now the challenge would come or the gun would roar. Bob wet his dry lips. He closed his eyes to compose himself. The schooner was bobbing up and down like a rocking horse. Was it the motion that was making him feel sick again? That was ridiculous. He had weathered many a storm in the Aleutians aboard the old *Otter* and if one didn't get sick in *those* waters, he'd never get sick anywhere else.

The flare died out and blackness closed in. The schooner plunged deeply again and again and then the motion eased and Bob felt a different, strong current grip the old hull.

" We've made it," said Keene. " Sibutu Passage."

" Look east! " called Gary.

Faintly, ever so faintly, almost indistinguishable, a pale line showed in the eastern sky, heralding the coming dawn.

" All hands on deck! " roared Chief Daly. " Let's make sail! "

The blocks creaked as the men sweated up the patched and discolored sails. They filled in the fresh breeze. The engine was throttled low. The old schooner settled down for a comfortable run away from the coming dawn.

" Australia! Here we come! " said Lieutenant Keene.

Bob smiled wanly. He remembered seeing a chart in the *Grayfin's* conning tower. They were in Sibutu Passage heading for the Celebes Sea. Once there they would have the choice of turning south toward Makassar Strait between Borneo and Celebes to reach the Java Sea, thence into the Flores Sea to round Timor into the Timor Sea, and then heading for Australia. The other choice would be to sail due east into the rising sun into the Celebes Sea

126

and to turn southerly off Morotai to try to reach New Guinea or continue on into the Bismarck Archipelago. That would be somewhat less mileage, but not much less, and besides, many of those islands were in Japanese hands. Those seas were patrolled by enemy surface, undersea, and air craft. Either way they went they would be traveling most of the way in Japanese-controlled waters.

The sky turned grayer and then gained in pinkish tinge. The schooner heeled in the freshening breeze, diving deeply now and then to send up a shower of spray. She sailed well for all her slatternly, down-at-the-heels appearance.

The smell of cooking food drifted to Bob and he suddenly realized he had not eaten a thing since leaving *Grayfin*. Bert Campbell stuck his head out of the scuttle. "We'll have your breakfast in a jiffy, cobber," he said with a wide smile. "Luverly dy, ain't it, mite?"

Bob grinned. Try to down an Australian!

Gary came aft, swaying with the motion of the schooner. "This old *Stinky Maru* isn't such a bad sea boat," he said.

The rising sun picked out something bright high in the sky. It was a plane wheeling in the sunlight. Far across the passage a thread of smoke arose from something. Perhaps a Japanese patrol craft. It was going to be a busy day in Sibutu Passage.

11

The bright sunlight sparkled from the moving waters. The waves seemed to be surging along on a journey that had no beginning and no ending. Spray dashed from the tops of a few of them and white wave horses pranced from one side of the passage to the other.

Stinky Maru plowed along to the steady thudding of the pumps, while a stream of dirty, rusty water flowed over the side to stain the blue waters. Those who weren't otherwise occupied were cleaning their weapons. The Australians had garnered three Japanese automatic rifles, half a dozen Nambu automatic pistols, and a case of Japanese grenades. The crew of the *Stinky Maru* could give a good account of themselves with the average small patrol boat, providing it was not armed with a deck gun. In that case the enemy could stand off at leisure and blow them out of the water.

Somewhere below the surface of the water might be *Grayfin* if nothing had happened to her. Perhaps she was still in the passage, or perhaps she had run for home. Perhaps her broken hull lay at the bottom of the passage with curious fish already probing into the shattered compartments, with an eye to finding a new home.

Several pairs of binoculars had been found aboard the schooner and Keene set a full-time watch using the powerful glasses. The men were amazed at the excellence of the instruments. Anything that moved upon the surface of the passage was scanned by keen eyes through the glasses. Several times fishing craft were spotted, mainly the sampan type, but now and then a large craft was seen, not much different from the *Stinky Maru*. There was a good radio set in the schooner's cabin. The receiver had been turned on and constant messages streamed through it, although the static was so bad none of the commandos could make out more than a few words.

The sun reached its zenith with nothing bothering *Stinky Maru*, but an hour later, a large fishing craft came up behind them, driven by a powerful engine. She altered her course half a mile behind the schooner.

Lieutenant Keene studied the oncoming craft. " Everyone below but the helmsman and lookout," he ordered.

The decks were cleared. Bob looked back over his shoulder. The fishing boat had a bone in her teeth. Spray showered back from her plunging bows.

" She's got a lot of antenna on her," said the officer, almost as though to himself. " Plenty of power too."

Bob looked away from the fishing craft. He glanced down at his loaded automatic pistol. Something Lieutenant Keene had said before they left the cove came back into his mind. " *My lads and I don't intend to surrender,*" he had said.

" I can't tell if she's got a deck gun," said the officer, " but there's something on her foredeck."

" If she comes alongside," said Bert Campbell from the scuttle, " we can jump her, dump this case of grenades down her hatch, and take off."

" And have every patrol boat and plane in the area come around to find out why she's sinking," said Keene. " Besides, she's got a lot of radio aboard her. Long-range stuff too, from the amount of it. She might get a message off before we could take care of her. That would be all we'd need right about now."

Bob could hear the throbbing of the powerful engine of the overhauling craft. He did not dare look around. His face was tanned and dirty and he had bound an old faded piece of cloth about his dark red hair. It was so dirty they'd never notice the color of it unless they were very close to him. He hoped they wouldn't be that curious. He reached down and covered the automatic pistol with a scrap of canvas and placed a bare foot atop the canvas. The heavy weapon felt slightly comforting under his foot.

" She's closing in," said Keene. " How do I look? "

Bob glanced at him. He too had dressed in the non-descript clothing of a fisherman and had bound a cloth about his thick black hair. Dirt and sun had tanned his lean face. Bob hoped he was as good in Japanese and the local native tongue as he said he was. " You'll do," said Bob. " You better get rid of that wristwatch though."

Keene stripped off the watch and dropped it into his pocket. His tommy gun lay at his feet covered with a coil of rope. Down in the cabin seven tough customers sat in silence, armed to the teeth and determined not to be taken alive. Bob suddenly felt like a target at a carnival booth on Saturday night.

The sound of the motor was very close now and the rushing of the bow wave would be heard. *Stinky Maru* wallowed and waddled along. An alien-sounding voice hailed the schooner.

Keene's whole personality and features seemed to change. He smiled, flashing a set of pure white teeth. He spoke quickly. Bob could see the bows of the other boat

130

rising and falling thirty feet off the port quarter of the schooner. He felt his throat go dry and brassy and an uneasy feeling settled in the pit of his stomach. Gary had squatted on the deck. He was too tall for the average native.

The harsh voice rattled on and on, Keene answered politely, with many bowings of the head.

The other boat pulled up farther until Bob could see a knot of hard-faced men standing on her foredeck. There was something behind them shielded in soiled canvas, but whether it was a deck gun or not he could not tell.

They moved up farther, and he could see more men standing in her low waist amid a tangle of gear. The men on the foredeck were looking keenly at *Stinky Maru* and her little crew.

Above the sound of the bigger boat's motor and the splashing and gurgling of the sea about the two boats came another sound. Bob looked up. The sun was flashing from the wings of a float plane that was diving repeatedly at something in the water on the far side of the passage. The men on the other boat turned to watch it. Again and again the plane dived. Bob could not hear machine-gun fire, of course, and he couldn't see whether or not the plane was firing.

For a long moment or two the boats coursed alongside each other, and then a man came from an after cabin, pointed to the plane and shouted in Japanese. Orders rattled on the deck of the bigger boat and she sheered off and plowed toward the plane and its unseen target. Smaller and smaller became the boat.

"Stay below!" Keene ordered. "They might have glasses on us!" He wiped the sweat from his dirty face.

"What was that all about?" said Bob.

131

Keene sat down on the rail and bowed his head to hold it in his hands, as though it was ready to split. " They asked if we had seen a suspicious craft out here, and I said no, that we hadn't. They asked why we hadn't received any message to that effect, and I said our radio wasn't working right. They offered to send a man over to fix it. That was about the time that plane acted up. Thank God for miracles! "

" We must have looked the part," said Bob. " You should have been an actor, sir."

Keene raised his head and looked wearily at Bob. " I was, laddie, I was. That's how I happened to be asked to volunteer for this mission. By the Lord Harry, I wish I was treading the boards again! "

The other boat was hull down when the rest of the men came up on deck. Bert Campbell lighted a cigarette. He flipped the match overboard. " Thank God they got interested in whatever was over there. This is one time I don't mind someone else getting it in the neck instead of us."

Red Kelly looked at Bob. Bob looked at the plane. The sun was still flashing from its wings. Suddenly a plume of water shot up into the air and right after it came a dull booming sound.

" *Grayfin*," said Kelly quietly.

Daly shot a look at him. " If you haven't got something sensible to say," he snapped, " don't say it! "

It was no use. It was in the minds of every one of the men of the *Grayfin* aboard the *Stinky Maru*.

" Was that patrol boat carrying depth charges? " asked Slim Polk.

Bob almost opened his mouth and then he shut it. He had seen what he thought looked like depth charges strung along the stern of the patrol boat. Maybe they had been extra fuel drums. Maybe . . .

A dull booming sound came across the passage, and a mound of water raised itself. The hull of the schooner trembled violently. Again and again the mounds of water arose, and again and again the *Stinky Maru* shuddered with the water pressure driven across the straits toward her. No one had to answer Slim's question. The answer was plain enough.

The schooner plunged on. There were long hours of daylight ahead of her and she was a long way from the mouth of the passage. Bob was relieved from the wheel and he went below to eat and then to try to sleep, but it was almost impossible. His uneasiness wasn't due to the motion of the schooner or the foul stench of her, or the greasy food he had eaten. It was the sight of those evil-looking mounds of water rising up from the depths and the shuddering impact of the water pressure against the old schooner that kept running through his mind.

What had been the target of those depth charges? Commander Currie had never mentioned any other American submarines on patrol in those perilous waters. There was something he had said that came back to Bob. *Three attempts have already been made by submarines to pick them up. All of them failed. This time they picked the right boat. Grayfin will not fail.*

The afternoon dragged on as *Stinky Maru* headed for the Celebes Sea. Regularly planes passed back and forth along the passage. Boats could be seen in the distance, but whether they were patrol boats or fishing boats was impossible to tell. The radio in the cabin of the schooner rasped and buzzed, with a few words coming through, and then they would die away.

Lieutenant Keene raised his head from his bunk as the

radio crackled and hummed. Words came through with startling clarity. The officer thrust his legs out of the bunk and sat up. He rubbed his tousled hair. " I have the strangest feeling they're trying to contact us," he said at last.

" Nobody bothering us by air or sea," said Red Kelly.

" No," said Keene quietly, " but we don't know if the *Stinky Maru* was only a fishing vessel, a patrol boat, or perhaps just a small transport. There's one thing certain. She's been missed by now and *somebody* must have found out what has happened back at the cove."

Bob looked up the scuttle. It was a long way until dusk and even that wouldn't be of much help with planes dropping parachute flares and patrol boats using radar and sonar gear.

" I wish we knew the code number of this bucket," said Chief Daly. " I've looked all through this cabin and couldn't find anything that looked like it."

" So even if we knew it," said Krasnowski, " what could we do with it? They'd get wise right off."

" Plane hanging around over us," said Bert Campbell from the deck. " Keeps passing back and forth. You can see somebody in the greenhouse watching us through a pair of glasses."

The radio crackled viciously. All eyes turned to it.

" I'll bet that's him," said Red Kelly.

Bob climbed up the ladder to the deck. A twin float patrol plane was swinging back and forth, banking steeply so that the observer could study them through his glasses. The plane circled and came back. A signal light flashed from the cockpit.

" Read it, kid," said Chief Daly dryly.

" I don't like this," said Tim Harkness.

They watched the plane circling and banking with the

insistent flashing of the light. The radio had stopped crackling.

" What do we do now? " said Tad Jones.

" Sit it out," said Chief Daly grimly. He looked up at the sky. " It's a long way until darkness."

For half an hour the plane hung around, sometimes swinging low enough so that they could see the faces of the pilot and the observer and then the plane, after a last insistent signaling, flew off toward the island.

Bert Campbell spat over the side. " It won't be long now," he said.

An hour before dusk Gary spotted a patrol craft moving toward them. There was no mistaking her through the binoculars. She was about the size of a United States Navy coastal mine sweeper, with high, flared bows and much antenna. Deck guns were plain to be seen and depth charges were racked at her squat stern. She looked fast, businesslike, and tough. Too tough for the little *Stinky Maru* sagging her way toward the Celebes Sea.

The radio snapped and crackled insistently.

" She's trying to reach us," said Daly. " No doubt about that, mates."

" Plane," said Gary.

It was the same curious character who had been circling them before. This time he flew straight toward them, swung low, and boomed past at mast-top level. This time the observer had pushed back the greenhouse cover and had swung out a pair of machine guns.

" Another patrol boat," said Tim Harkness quietly.

This one was coming from the other side of the passage, throwing up showers of spray as she was pushed into the seas. She was smaller than the first one, but still able to take care of the *Stinky Maru*.

Lieutenant Keene looked about at his motley crew. "You Yanks know how we commandos stand," he said. "We'll have to fight. If you like, you can take the small boat. They'll pick you up."

"I'll bet they will," said Krasnowski. He reached under a piece of canvas and patted his BAR. "I'm sticking aboard."

Chief Daly looked about. His face winced in pain. He had aged considerably in the short time since he had left *Grayfin*. He looked up at the plane and then at the two approaching boats. "None of you lads have to stay," he said. "But I am. I'd never survive their beatings and their rotten prison camps."

Bob looked at Gary. They were between the devil and the deep blue sea; they were damned if they did and damned if they didn't. Gary rubbed his hand across his eyes. "We haven't much choice or chance," he said.

Tim Harkness checked his weapons. "Best bet is to play dumb and let them close. If they stand off, they can shell us out of the blinking water."

Stinky Maru wallowed peacefully on. The men not needed on the deck went below. Bob took the wheel and Gary acted again as lookout while Lieutenant Keene busied himself about the deck. Once more the radio crackled. Then it went dead. A signal light flashed from the biggest of the two boats, steadily and insistently, again and again. The same letters, although Bob had no idea what the signal was or what they wanted in return.

"Fortunes of war," said the officer.

"I never believed we'd get away with it," said Bob.

The officer looked at him. "Always keep trying, Bob. Never give up." He smiled. "Don't give up the ship!"

Bob didn't have the heart to smile back.

136

The signal lamp blinked out. There was a flash of flame and a puff of smoke and something hummed through the air. A splash materialized in front of the schooner. The meaning was plain enough. *Heave to!*

Lieutenant Keene and Gary let the patched, faded sails fall at a run, billowing and flapping to cover the decks and the main cabin. They might help conceal the men hidden below, but it wasn't likely.

Bob looked at the two boats. They were each within three hundred yards of the schooner, approaching from the stern and from either side. The plane banked and flew low. The dying sun glistened bloodily from the plane's wings. In another hour the schooner might have escaped under cover of darkness. She wallowed helplessly in the pitching seas.

Bob released the useless wheel and let it spin. He looked longingly at the small boat, but that wouldn't be of much help. They couldn't all get into it and they certainly couldn't escape in it. This was the end.

The larger of the two boats moved in closer and a voice rattled at them across the gap between the two boats. Keene made a gesture as though he couldn't hear plainly. If only they came in closely enough to take a crack at them, but a BAR, a few submachines and pistols, and a case of grenades could hardly overcome either one of the boats.

A small boat was lowered from the larger patrol boat and a dozen seamen tumbled into it, carrying rifles. It turned toward the schooner, and oars began to stroke rhythmically pulling the boat through the pitching waves.

"Maybe we could grab off those boys and use them as hostages," said Slim Polk from the engine room hatch. "They wouldn't shoot at us then."

"Don't delude yourself," said Keene. "If they want us badly enough, they won't hesitate to shoot on their own men."

The sun was low, casting a curious-colored pattern on the water. It was almost impossible to see anything toward the mouth of the passage.

The plane swung far out and turned again back toward the three vessels heaving on the water. The small boat was so close to the schooner that Bob could see the hard face of the officer in the stern sheets beside the man at the tiller.

Something boomed to the south of the three boats. There was a rushing sound in the air and a plume of water and spray shot high in front of the bows of the largest patrol boat. The booming sound came again and something slammed into the bows of the larger boat with frightful force, hurling men and gear over the side. Three times more the sound came and each time the boat was savagely struck. The deck was lifted from the shattered planking as though by an invisible hand and hurled into the sea. A bright tongue of flame ran across the deck.

The Japanese in the pulling boat had stopped rowing. They stared openmouthed toward the setting sun, but there was nothing they could see. Again and again the shells screamed out of the glare. Suddenly there was a dull roaring sound that grew in volume and the middle of the patrol boat rose and blasted into the smoky air, hurling timbers, gear, and men high into the air to splash into the sea.

"Now!" yelled Lieutenant Keene. He leaned across the sagging rail of the schooner and emptied a full drum of cartridges into the small boat. Men shrieked and screamed. Some of them fired back. Others fell into the sea or jumped

138

into it. Big Krasnowski opened fire with his BAR and when he was done the boat was a shattered, sinking wreck with a few men swimming about it.

There was nothing left of the larger boat but a mass of shattered smoking timbers heaving on the red-lit waters. The smaller boat had turned away, zigzagging to escape, but again the booming sound came and a shell struck the rear of her charthouse, opening it out like a house of cards. She turned aimlessly to starboard, and three shells tacked a battering line of fire down her sides.

The plane came roaring in low, heading for the mysterious source of the deadly shooting, but he made one fatal mistake. He flew at masthead height right over the *Stinky Maru,* and everything from automatic pistols, a BAR, tommy guns, and Japanese automatic rifles opened up on him. He seemed to get caught upon an invisible rope stretched across the straits. The nose swung up and the plane seemed to hang in the air to drop sideways. Another hail of fire caught her. She blew apart with a dull, roaring sound that echoed across the heaving waters. A brilliant ball of incandescent gas appeared for a few seconds and then there was nothing but thick smoke in the air as the few fragments of the plane splashed into the sea.

" They never will armor their planes or install self-sealing gas tanks," said Chief Daly. He grounded the Nambu automatic rifle he had emptied into the plane. " Maybe we ought to paint a meatball on the side of the old *Stinky Maru.*"

" Look! Look! " screamed Gary.

They all turned to see a submarine moving quickly toward them, the seas flowing back from her scabrous black sides, encrusted with salt sores and streaks of rust. Life-jacketed, helmeted men stood about the deck gun, and automatic weapons pointed upward toward the darkening sky.

"I hope that's the blinkin' *Grayfin*," said Tim Harkness.

"It's the blinkin' *Grayfin*, all right," said Chief Daly.

Swiftly the submarine closed the gap until she was heaving gently up and down with the water flowing along her dark sides and through her freeing ports. "Chief Daly!" hailed a familiar voice. "You've got five minutes to scuttle that bait barge and get aboard *Grayfin* where you belong!"

"Aye, aye, Commander!" yelled Daly.

Men opened the rusty sea cocks while others got the small boat over the side. By the time the first load had been taken to *Grayfin*, the *Stinky Maru* was slowly settling. By the time the last load reached the submarine, the schooner was deck-deep in the water.

Bob scrambled aboard *Grayfin* with a prayer of thanksgiving in his heart. He looked out over the darkening seas. Flotsam and jetsam heaved up and down on the waves. Half a dozen Japanese stood on what remained of part of the deck of the smaller patrol boat. Slowly *Grayfin* moved toward them with a throbbing of diesels and a barking of exhausts.

Browning automatic rifles and tommy guns covered the men on the fragment of deck. They stood there, stripped to the skin, stolidly wringing the water out of their soaked clothing.

"Who speaks Japanese?" said Commander Currie.

"I do, sir," said Lieutenant Keene.

"Tell them to come aboard. They will be well treated as prisoners of war under the rules of the Geneva Convention," said the skipper.

Keene took the megaphone and spoke through it to the

men. There was no expression on their faces. They did not speak.

The wind was picking up. The fragment of deck sank lower. Waves began to wash about the ankles of the men. Bob looked at the rising seas. A dark triangular thing cut through water and vanished. Beyond where it had vanished, there appeared another and another. " Sharks! " yelled a lookout.

" We haven't much time," said the skipper. " I'm endangering my boat every second I stay on the surface."

Keene spoke again. He pleaded. He commanded. He pointed toward the evil-looking fins that were encircling the raft. As one man the Japanese turned their backs on the submarine. The water began to wash about their calves.

"Sound contact, bridge! " rasped the speaker. " High-speed screws! More than one vessel! Bearing three-three-oh! Moving very fast, sir! "

Currie bit his lip. He looked at Keene. " Try again," he said.

" It's no use, sir."

" Radar contact! " said the speaker. " Three pips bearing three-three-oh! Coming fast! Destroyers, sir! Range ten thousand yards, sir! "

" That does it! All below! " Currie ordered. " Lookouts below! Clear the bridge! Dive! Dive! Dive! "

They tumbled down the ladder one atop the other. The diving klaxon sounded and the submarine slanted downward. The diesels died away and the electrics took over. Deeper and deeper went *Grayfin* into her elements. The hatch was slammed shut and secured by Commander Currie. The vents had been opened and water was pouring into the tanks. Water was already pouring around the bridge plating and flowing over the hatch. In sixty seconds *Grayfin* was completely submerged, leaving only a little swirling foam on the darkened sea to mark her passage. Eighteen hundred tons, more than three hundred feet long, plunged down toward deeper water.

"Fast screws!" called the sonarman. "Close aboard starboard beam!"

Deeper and deeper went *Grayfin*. "Rig for silent running," said Commander Currie.

Gary Lunt got down on the deck and kissed the wet oily surface, and one after the other, under the amused eyes of the commandos every one of the shore party, including Chief Daly, did exactly the same thing.

Thrum-thrum-thrum-thrum sounded the screws right overhead, and the hull of the submarine shook with the savage sound. *Chow-chow-chow-chow* they sounded until it seemed as though the spinning bronze blades were actually tearing into the deck above the listening men. Slowly it passed on and on until it was no more than a faint humming. The screws had slowed down.

"She's echo-ranging, sir," said the sonarman.

Lieutenant Davis flipped on the speaker switch. The high-pitched pinging of the Japanese sound gear came through the speaker. *Peep . . . peep . . . peeeeeeep . . . peeep . . . peep.*

"Sounds like a bloomin' canary," said Tim Harkness.

The men in the control room exploded into laughter.

Slowly, ever so slowly, the sound died away, until it was gone. "Lost contact, sir," said the sonarman.

"Periscope depth," came the command.

Grayfin slanted up and Commander Currie took a periscope look-see. "Completely dark now," he said. "We'll run submerged until we are clear of the passage and then

142

surface to approach Tawitawi." He slapped up the training handles of the periscope. " Down scope! " He looked about the control room. " You gentlemen know we have a two-fold mission. We have accomplished the first part of that mission." He turned on the speaker. " Now hear this! In order to achieve the first part of our mission we have had to use stealth and could not fight back until it was necessary to pick up our commando friends and the shore party. Our mission now is to scout the major Japanese Fleet Operating Base at Tawitawi. That we will do. One more thing: there is nothing in my instructions that states we cannot operate as a fighting craft of the United States Navy. That we will do! That is all."

The cheering that broke loose in the submarine could conceivably have been heard by a surface craft, but *Grayfin* and her crew did not care. They were on their way to strike a blow against Japanese surface craft. From all the reports about Tawitawi there would be plenty of Japanese ships there ready for the reaping.

12

GRAYFIN hung just below the surface of the moonlit sea with her periscope up while Commander Currie studied the approaches to Tawitawi. Since sunset *Grayfin* had hovered about the approaches, rising at times to periscope depth, diving swiftly if A/S craft were seen or propeller sounds were picked up by the sonarman. Conditions were quite different off Tawitawi. Instead of small auxiliary craft, perhaps converted trawlers or fishermen acting as A/S patrols, the Japanese had spread a net of destroyers off Tawitawi. Hardly an hour passed without sonar picking up high-speed screws, and now and then the sound of echo-ranging. The reports passed on throughout the skulking submarine indicated that there was plenty of activity off Tawitawi. Tankers and supply ships approached the great anchorage or left protected by full destroyer escort and with float planes providing an air umbrella.

There was one thing the men of *Grayfin* knew. The Imperial Japanese Navy was desperately short of two types of craft necessary to carry on a successful naval war. Tankers and destroyers. Tawitawi was well supplied with both types, and information supplied to Commander Currie before he left Brisbane had indicated that both types traveled in each other's company. Some reconnaissance reports had stated that it was not uncommon for a lone, high-speed tanker to have a destroyer all to itself, and sometimes as many as three tin cans escorted the vital craft. It was a good indication that despite their lack of destroyers, they were more concerned with tankers and their precious fuel. That fuel was the lifeblood of the Imperial Japanese Mobile Fleet at Tawitawi.

The men of *Grayfin* knew something else. They cast thoughtful looks at Commander Currie if they saw him, or when they heard his terse talks over the sound system they eyed the speakers just as thoughtfully. Gil Currie had never indicated how difficult it had been for him to pass by that small convoy when *Grayfin* was running in toward Sibutu Passage to pick up the commandos. There were other memories that rankled in the skipper's mind. In order to reach that rendezvous within the required time he had been forced to drive *Grayfin* to her limit, keeping out of the way of enemy surface ships, prime targets for a submarine that had returned a number of times to her base with a broom lashed to her periscopes, and with strings of Japanese meatball flags snapping in the wind, indicating she had swept the seas of enemy vessels in *Grayfin's* patrol area. There had been some talk of *maru* fever among the crew of the *Grayfin,* and the death of likable Dusty Fuller by an accident that might have been easily prevented had not set well with crew. Now *Grayfin* lay off Tawitawi, with not a torpedo expended, and only a handfull of shells had been used from the deck gun. The next move was that of Commander Currie.

" Propeller sounds bearing three-oh-oh," reported sonar. " Fading away. Moving slowly."

" Up scope! " snapped the skipper, riding the training handles up as the long instrument whined up out of its deep well. He peered through the scope. " Moonlight," he said thoughtfully. " Cloudy though. Patches of moonlight and patches of darker areas where the clouds are." His voice died away.

Grayfin moved slowly through the depths with her operating noises blended together. The humming of the electric motors and the mingled mutterings of the bow and stern motors were working to keep *Grayfin* at periscope depth.

" Propeller sounds dying away," reported sonar. There was a moment or two of concentration on the sonarman's face. " Gone completely now."

Slowly *Grayfin* moved closer to shore. " Nips are certainly cocky," said the skipper. " I can see lights on shore. Like diamonds. Patrol boat anchored with deck lights on."

" How big? " asked Lieutenant Olson.

" Not big enough to make it worthwhile for us to reveal ourselves," said the skipper.

Tom Olson looked at Mack Davis. Davis wiped the sweat from his face. Well, he had wanted action. What was the skipper looking for?

" Faint propeller sounds. Bearing two-seven-two," reported sonarman Scarlotti.

Currie swung the scope to the bearing and studied the area. " Nothing," he said.

" Becoming louder," said sonar. " Approaching at low speed, sir."

Currie peered through the scope. " Down scope!" he said. The scope slid down into its well. " Dive to ninety feet! "

The sub slanted forward as the planes were worked. " We'll dive under him," Currie said.

" What was it, sir? " Ensign Tolliver asked.

" Hard to tell. It wasn't a destroyer though. What's the depth here, Tom? "

" Three hundred and fifty, sir."

Currie nodded. *Grayfin* leveled off at ninety feet. She slid easily through the water. The sound of the propellers came louder, seemingly heading right for the submerged boat. " Rig for silent running," commanded the skipper.

" He's changed his course, sir," said Scarlotti. " Speeding up a bit."

" He's feeling about for us," said Currie.

" He's echo-ranging, sir," said the sonarman.

A faint *thrum-thrum-thrum* sounded and then the ominous *ping-g-g-g ping-g-g-g ping-g-g-g-g* came echoing through the speaker. Louder and louder it came and then it slowly faded away. Another sound overlaid the first. *Peep . . . peep . . . peeeeeep . . . peeeep peeep . . . peeep . . . peep.*

" Another one," said Scarlotti. " Bearing one-eight-oh. Sounds different from the first one."

The motors were stopped and *Grayfin* was allowed to sink deeper into the water. The peeping sound intensified, then faded away and died altogether.

" Faint propeller noises, fading away," said Scarlotti.

" One or two A/S? " asked the skipper.

" One, sir. Almost gone now."

The sound died out of the speaker altogether.

Eyes flicked upward as though they could see through the steel hull of the submerged boat and to the surface of the sea where the A/S craft were working.

Commander Currie rubbed his jaw. " We're well out of the entrance channel," he said. " They might have mistaken us for a wreck. On the other hand, they've probably got every wreck charted accurately."

147

Minutes ticked past as *Grayfin* floated there in her liquid world, like a bird hovering motionless in the sky, upheld by the updraft. There was no further sound from the sonar speaker.

An hour passed before the motors were started and *Grayfin* rose slowly to periscope depth. Slowly the periscope was revolved. "All clear," said the skipper. He slapped the training handles. He looked around the hot, damp control room, studying each man's face. "How about a little fresh air?" he asked.

"Lookouts to the control room!" came the command.

Bob leaped up from his bunk and pulled on his shoes. He punched Gary on the arm. "Come on, Big Eyes," he said. "We need you on deck tonight as we've never needed you before!"

Grayfin broke the moonlit surface of the sea and in a matter of seconds the bridge watch was standing on the alert. It was a rather eerie, uncanny panorama that was presented to the men on the bridge and those who hung in the lookout rings, scanning the sea with their powerful glasses. Tawitawi was plain to be seen, bathed in full moonlight with lights scattered here and there and some in concentrations. The moonlight glittered from the water and shone down on the Japanese vessels that looked like minatures on the rippling water of the outer harbor. But where *Grayfin* moved slowly on the surface, it was dark beneath a thick layer of drifting clouds. *Grayfin* recharged batteries and pumped air into the flasks.

There wasn't a sign of enemy surface craft. After all the Japanese A/S activity while *Grayfin* had been submerged, the contrast was rather startling. Bob swung his glasses. It didn't seem possible to him that they would suddenly quit and allow *Grayfin* to surface. He glanced at Gary,

148

and saw him shake his head.

The sonar was working and the radar antenna swung steadily while each of the four lookouts scanned the waters and the sky. It was as though the Japanese had suddenly decided to knock off for the night and go home.

" Slow-speed screws bearing three-oh-oh, sir! " rasped the squawk box on the bridge.

Bob swung his glasses. There was a darkness out there like a thicker patch of shadow. He couldn't tell if it was moving or not.

" Radar," asked Commander Currie, " haven't you anything? "

" Nothing, sir. I'm afraid we've got trouble, sir," answered the radarman.

" Get cracking on it," the skipper said. " I don't want to be without radar in these waters."

" Screws coming closer," said sonar. " Sound peculiar. I've never heard anything quite like this before."

" Switch it on," said the skipper.

The sound came through the speaker, a curiously intermingled sound. The visual lookouts could see nothing in the direction of the vessel. She was traversing a course that would bring her across the bows of the submarine at about three thousand yards. Prime for a spread of torpedoes.

" It's not a destroyer," said the skipper in a puzzled voice.

" More likely a small supply vessel," said Mack Davis. " She's moving awfully slow and certainly isn't echo-ranging."

" Might have radar," said the skipper thoughtfully.

It added to the eeriness of the night. Moving patches of shadows drifted across the rippling waters. Here and

149

there were broad patches where the moon completely lighted the surface of the sea.

The sound of the screws slowed down perceptibly. "She's barely on steerage way," said Mack Davis.

The skipper turned his glasses in the direction of the surface craft. "Might be waiting for a pilot," he said.

"Out there with a chance one of our boats might be waiting for her?" asked the exec. "Doesn't make sense, Gil."

The sound of the diesel exhausts sounded inordinately loud to Bob, but they needed life-giving air in the flasks and the only way they could get it was through the diesels running on the surface.

"All stop," said the skipper.

The engine room annunciators tinkled. The diesels died away. The water rippled against the hull of the submarine. Faintly, ever so faintly, came a sound from the land. There was nothing in sight except the lights and there were less of them than there had been before. There wasn't a sound of a patrolling plane or the sound of a patrolling boat. Nothing but those screws barely turning over.

"We'll take a look-see," said the commander.

Grayfin poked her bullnose into the shadows. She needed radar now as never before, but there was no report from the radarman that he had located the trouble.

Then the squawk box was silent. "Are you getting anything at all, Scarlotti?" asked the skipper.

"Nothing, sir. She's stopped."

Grayfin moved on. The exhausts sounded loud enough to be heard ashore, thought Bob.

The sound of the screws came again through the squawk box. "She's moving on the same course, sir."

Currie commanded a change in course to angle in toward the unseen ship. *Grayfin* felt her way along.

"Maybe she's having engine trouble," suggested Mack Davis. "She doesn't sound quite the same as she did before."

Bob scanned the dark sea. The moon had vanished behind the thick clouds. The executive officer was right. The sound was *not* the same as it had been before. Bob had had enough experience as sonarman striker in his time aboard *Grayfin* to learn quite a bit from Jack Scarlotti.

"Beats me," said the skipper. "I wish we were fully charged."

The sound became louder and again changed its timbre. There was more of an intermingling of sounds now. "Sounds like *two* of them, sir," said the sonarman.

Bob raised his glasses. He looked off into the darkness. There *was* something out there. He opened, then closed his mouth. He didn't want to make any mistakes. As Commander Currie had once said, there wasn't any room on a submarine for mistakes.

"Sounds like high-speed screws! It is!" snapped Scarlotti.

Bob swallowed hard. Suddenly he saw a V-shaped whiteness. For one frozen moment he couldn't speak. "Destroyer!" he shouted. "Bearing two-seven-oh! Coming fast!"

Currie slammed his hand onto the handle of the diving klaxon and drove it full to the stops. The piercing *aaaa-oooo-gaaa, aaaa-oooo-gaaa, aaaa-oooo-gaaa* of the diving alarm reverberated throughout the boat. "Lookouts below!" yelled the skipper. "Clear the bridge! *Dive! Dive! Dive!*"

The last thing Bob saw as he fled for the open hatchway

151

was an ominous V of luminous white spray approaching the submarine at tremendous speed. The men rode down the ladder virtually on each other's shoulders as the submarine crash-dived. The hatch slammed shut and was locked. Water roared into the ballast tanks and the speed dropped from eight to five knots. The diesels died away and the electrics drove *Grayfin* downward.

"All ahead emergency! Two hundred feet! Rig for depth charge! Rig for silent running!" ripped out the tense commands.

The diving seemed to have a maddening slowness. *Grayfin*, in common with her sister boats, had a tendency to "hang" on a dive at thirty-five feet.

The throb, throb, throbbing noise came from the outside of the hull, steadily and rapidly increasing in pitch and tempo — *thum-thum-thum-thum-THUM-THUM!*

Fans, electric motors, and air-conditioning machinery had been cut off. The boat was being worked by hand controls. Shoes were pulled off so as not to make noises on the steel decks.

The depth gauge needle broke the thirty-five-foot mark at last.

THUM - THUM - THUM - THUM - THUM - THUM drummed through the sinking hull.

Forty feet . . . forty-five feet . . . fifty feet . . . *Grayfin* was making it, but not a split second too soon. The drumming pounding noise of the destroyer's spinning screws roared unbearably through the hull.

Sixty feet . . . sixty-five feet . . . seventy feet . . . Men looked at each other and grinned weakly.

Grayfin began to worm her way beneath the dark waters, trying to shake off that maddening, persistent sound.

There was a noise as of two heavy coffee cups being

152

knocked together sounding clearly. A heavy explosion rocked the sinking boat. Light bulbs winked out abruptly. Glass tinkled. White cork flakes from the bulkhead insulation drifted down like snowflakes. A weird rushing sound mingled with the thudding of the destroyer's screws as tons of water turned over on the submarine's superstructure.

The clicking sound came again, followed by a thudding noise and a swishing sound and *Grayfin* staggered as the depth charge drove tons and tons of water at her. Each time it sounded as though some underwater giant was slamming a gigantic sledge hammer against the side of the boat. Men were hurled to the decks or staggered on their feet. The whole hull seemed to whip as depth charge after depth charge let go, mingled all the time with that maddening *THUM-THUM-THUM-THUM-THUM.*

Somewhere within the straining hull frames bent a little. Piping, ventilation lines and other gear set up a strong sympathetic vibration. Light bulbs hung separated from overhead light fixtures by pieces of insulated wire. Dust and cork carpeted the deck.

The heat began to rise in the sub as she sank to one hundred feet. It hit 120 degrees. The ventilating and air conditioning had been shut off and they couldn't be turned on again until that maddened hornet buzzing around on the surface could be shaken off.

The clicks and the explosions came farther apart, indicating the destroyer had veered off in her mad, blind search for the submarine somewhere beneath her. If the clicks and explosions came closer together, she would be getting warm on the hunt again.

A bad leak was reported forward, but the pumps could not be started yet. *Grayfin* had reached two hundred feet and the great outside pressure was driving water into the boat in needlelike streams. The water was steadily rising in the forward bilges.

The sound of the destroyer's screws came back toward the submarine, a steady *schir-schir-schir-schir,* and then they faded away. *Grayfin* sank without propulsive power.

Ping ... ping ... pingg ... pingg ... pinggg ... pinggg ... pingggg ... pingggg ... pingggggg ... pinggggggg ... sounded through the sonar gear, filling the interior of the hull with a weird, high-pitched threnody. The tin can was echo-ranging. Then the sound was overlaid by a slightly different sound. There were two of them up there on the darkening sea feeling for *Grayfin* with their echo-ranging apparatus.

The crew stripped down to their skivvies, with soaked towels hanging around their necks. Sweat dripped down to join the water on the decks.

"Pump room is flooding!" came the hoarse cry from below the control room.

"How bad is it?" called out the exec.

One of the officers dived down the pump room hatch. "We can plug it," he called back. "A grease fitting in the negative tank flood valve operating gear carried away."

Commander Currie swabbed his face with a soaked towel. "All we need is to lose our pumps," he said.

"What's the difference?" said Mack Davis. "We can't use 'em anyway."

The skipper looked at him. "Sometimes," he said quietly, "sometimes . . ." He wearily shook his head.

"Water rising high in forward room bilges," came the report.

The skipper looked at the depth gauge. "Level her off at two hundred and fifty," he ordered.

154

The gauge sank steadily to two hundred and fifty feet.

Poing . . . poing . . . poingg . . . poingg . . . poinggg . . . poinggg . . . poingggg . . . poingggg . . . poinggggggg . . . poinggggggg . . . echoed from the speaker. All eyes turned upward, although they knew all they would see would be the overhead of the submarine. He was making contact!

The *thum-thum-thum-thum* came again. " Two of them, sir," said the sonarman.

THUM - THUM - THUM - THUM - THUM - THUM - THUM roared through the sinking submarine. The click-explosion-click-explosion came again and again. The *Grayfin* was shaken like a terrier shakes a rat. The air was filled with dust and fine particles of paint and cork. Ventilation lines and pipelines vibrated themselves out of sight. No man could stand on his feet. A motormac was knocked unconscious by leaning against a bulkhead. The lights flicked out and the bluish emergency lights came on. The heavy steel pressure bulkheads were squeezed in with each massive blow and sprang out again from their places. Pieces of equipment, valve handles, and tools were slammed about like deadly missiles.

The depth gauge needle hovered at three hundred feet and then dipped lower, and lower, *and lower.* . . . *Grayfin* was too heavy forward to level off. The forward room bilges were filling up and overflowing.

"Stern tube packing is leaking," came a tense report. "Motor room bilges filling up."

That was at the *other* end of the sinking submarine. The great depth was compressing the hull, increasing the buoyant volume. *Grayfin* was heavier by four tons. The pumps could not be started.

Click . . . WHAM! . . . Click . . . WHAM! . . . Click . . .

WHAM! . . . Click . . . WHAM! . . . Click . . . WHAM! . . . WHAM! WHAM! WHAM!WHAM!WHAM! WHAM!WHAM!WHAM! WHAM! So close together they could hardly be counted, but that didn't matter, for the fury of the moment was fully on the sinking boat. Deck plates were hurled about. The frames rang. *Grayfin* shook in every fiber of her metal being as though the depth charges were trying to separate the molecules and atoms that formed her fabrication. The men who gripped instruments and equipment, such as the bow and stern planes and steering, saw their knuckles go white with hand pressure. In the maneuvering room a thread of smoke arose but the fire was quickly spotted and put out.

The depth charging stopped. The sound of the screws moved away. The echo-ranging came again.

"They're looking for oil leaks or pieces of the boat," said Slim Polk to Bob and Gary. "Must be dark as pitch up there by now."

"All hands off duty form bucket brigades," came the voice of Mack Davis. "We've got to get the water out of those forward rooms. The leak has been stopped in the maneuvering room. We are gaining control of the leak in the motor room."

Buckets were issued and the sweating, gasping men began to bail water from the forward room back into the bilges of other rooms to try and trim the boat. She was at a ten- to twelve-degree angle. Sweat dripped from the faces and bodies of the men and the close, foul air made them gasp. When a man went over, the pharmacist did the best he could to bring him around. Chief Potter moved through the boat testing the air. Now and then he shook his head. They had hardly been surfaced long enough to recharge fully with air.

156

There were eighty-eight men in the boat, counting the commandos. The atmosphere tested at 2½ percent carbon dioxide. The danger line was 3 percent, and men fainted at that percentage. Death came at 4 percent.

Chief Potter spread CO_2 absorbent throughout the boat. Oxygen was released at regular intervals from oxygen bottles. That helped a little. It was the heat that got worse, especially for the men who were bailing out the bilges. Salt tablets were of little help. The decks ran with slippery perspiration. They and the bulkheads were literally alive with water. The humidity had climbed to a full 100 percent.

Gary dropped his bucket, and Bob deftly caught it so that it would not clang on the deck. Gary rolled up his eyes and fell sideways, then lay still.

The submarine began to creak and groan in the great pressure. The decks began to bulge slightly at their centers. Steadily the bucket brigade kept on. They were deep enough now so that it would almost be impossible for the Japanese to pick up any sound they would make. Slowly, ever so slowly, the submarine came back on an even keel.

"She'll sink with our sweat," said Red Kelly.

"Can't," said Bob cheerfully.

"Why not?" said Joe Krasnowski.

Bob wiped his streaming face. "We aren't adding any more weight than that which we brought aboard."

"Where's it all coming from?" asked Red.

"*That*," said Bob, "I can't answer."

"Stow that bailing," said Chief Potter.

Slowly, running silently, hand maneuvered by strong men who streamed perspiration, the *Grayfin* crept away like a wounded animal and rose to a less dangerous depth.

Now and then sonar picked up the sound of distant

screws, but none came close and the echo-ranging had died out.

Gary had come to. He lay on his bunk and looked weakly at Bob. " I turned chicken," he said.

" No fault of yours, pal," said Bob. He closed his eyes. His lungs felt as if they were on fire. His head throbbed and pounded.

" I say, Yanks," said Lieutenant Keene from another bunk, " any chance of taking us *back* to Borneo? "

" We've shaken them," said Slim Polk.

There was no sound coming from the sonar gear except some fish noises.

Chief Potter came through to the forward torpedo room. " Rest easy," he said. " Try to get some sleep. You need rest more than anything else. Conserves oxygen! "

She was running as silently as possible through the dark sea to get away from that place of exploding hell.

Bob closed his eyes. They never had had a chance to use any of their torpedoes. With vigilance such as that on the surface, they'd have little chance to surprise the enemy. " How do you suppose they worked that tin can up on us? " he asked.

Chief Potter leaned against Bob's bunk. " I've been fig- uring it out," he said. " There was nothing in sight up there when we surfaced. That was the come-on. They knew we were submerged and they also knew we had to come up to recharge batteries and air flasks. Then they had an old tub of a merchant ship lying somewhere out there with a tin can right beside it, on the far side. They picked us up and began to move together toward the harbor. Unluckily for us our radar had to go out at that time. First time it's ever happened on this boat. The merchant ship sounded so slow and uncertain because she was pulling that tin can

158

right alongside of her. Once we began to tail the ship at an angle, the destroyer cast loose, picked us up, and roared in to ram us or sink us by gunfire, figuring she'd get us that way, and that we couldn't get deep enough to protect ourselves against depth-charging."

" They were *nearly* right," said Bob.

" It was close all right," agreed the chief. He smiled. " In an hour or so we'll be far enough away to surface and air out this boat. Take it easy. Get some sleep. It's all over, fellows."

Bob closed his eyes again. He almost *thought* he could get some sleep.

" *Fire in the maneuvering room!* " rang through the submarine.

" Damage control party aft! " yelled Chief Potter.

Bob hit the deck. He raced aft behind the chief. The acrid smell of smoke was beginning to seep through the heated interior of the submarine.

13

S MOKE was swirling thickly through the forward engine room. Coughing, gagging men stood to their positions. Three damage control men waited for Chief Potter. One of them handed him a smoke mask. Bob took a smoke mask from another man. Potter ran into the after engine room, where the smoke was thicker, followed by his party. One of them closed the forward door of the room.

" Who's in there? " Potter asked Baldy, who was on duty in the room.

" Thomson, Goldberg, and Smith," said Baldy. " It's real bad, Chief. Water shorted out the battery switches. The wiring is blazing."

" Have they got smoke masks? " demanded Potter as he looked at the closed after door.

" Yes," said Baldy, " but they musta got a good dose of smoke before they got them on. I'm not so sure they're all right."

Potter nodded his head. He walked to the door and looked back at his crew. " I'm going in to take a look-see. If I'm not back in five minutes, you'll have to come in and get us. Understand? "

They all nodded. Potter undogged the watertight door and stepped quickly inside, closing the door behind him.

The smoke was drifting throughout the sub, but there

was nothing that could be done about it. Sweat streamed from the waiting men. Baldy pointed silently to a thermometer. It registered 115 degrees. Feet squelched on the water that flowed across the greasy deck.

"Three minutes," said Hank Burton quietly.

Bob felt as though he was going to get sick all over the diesels. Not a sound came from the maneuvering room.

"They can't live in there," said Baldy desperately. "You got to do something!"

"We've got our orders," said Chuck Schmidt.

"Four minutes," said Hank Burton. "Get ready. I'll open the door and go in first. Schmidt, you back me up. Dunbar and Meroff stand by the door. We'll have to move fast or we'll lose all those men."

"And the boat," said Baldy.

"Stow that!" snarled Ben Meroff. "We're not losing those men *or* the boat!"

"Time," said Hank. He opened the door and darted into the smoke-filled room followed by Chuck Schmidt. Bob and Ben moved close up beside the door. Hank appeared supporting a limp, coughing man. Bob and Ben grabbed the man and half dragged, half carried him to the forward door and through it into the forward engine room. Other men took the limp figure. Bob and Ben ran back in time to carry another unconscious man into the forward engine room. The thick smoke was billowing out of the open door, and the after engine room was filled with it. Bob never knew how many times he and Ben made the trip helping a semiconscious man or hauling an unconscious man through to comparative safety.

Chief Potter swayed in the doorway and fell face forward on the filthy deck of the engine room, dropping a fire extinguisher. The heat was a fearful, living thing.

Bob grabbed up the extinguisher and darted into the maneuvering room. It was a weird place, smoke-filled, with flickering dazzling blue sparks dancing above reddish-yellow flames. Bob worked the extinguisher beside Hank Burton and in a few minutes the fires were out, but the smoke was thicker than ever. They staggered out into the after engine room and slammed the door shut.

"Now what?" gasped Bob.

Burton shrugged. "We can't get this smoke out of here," he said hoarsely.

Baldy mopped his streaming face. "It's all over with us," he gasped, "unless we can surface."

"Now hear this," came the voice of Commander Currie through the boat. "You all know we are in a bad way. We can't last much longer down here. I propose to surface and fight it out with those tin cans up there, win, lose, or draw."

The weary, coughing, sweat-soaked men looked at each other. This just might mean the end of the line for *Grayfin*.

"Any objections must be written out in triplicate," continued the skipper. "I will personally see to it that the original and one copy will be forwarded to your congressman." There was a short pause. "I've had enough of this and so has *Grayfin! Stand by to surface!*"

Hoarse cheers resounded through the smoke-filled interior of the boat as men ran to their stations over the slimy, slippery decks. Better to die fighting on the surface, with the hope of taking a Japanese or two with you, than to die entombed far below the surface without being able to strike a blow.

Slowly the sluggish boat began to rise. It seemed like hours before she reached periscope depth. Sonar picked up the sound of a rain squall beating on the surface. Ten-

sion filled the foul interior of the submarine as the skipper
made a scope reconnaissance. No one spoke. No one dared
to think. There was only hope — hope that they wouldn't
have to go back into the living hell below them.

"Battle stations surface!" ordered Commander Currie.
"Stand by to surface!" The klaxon began to blare.

Minutes ticked past as *Grayfin* thrust herself upward
like a wounded whale. Commander Currie reached for the
conning tower hatch. He flung it open and as he did so
there was a howling rush of air throughout the boat. The
skipper was sucked up in the vortex without touching the
ladder. He stepped aside as he reached the deck, having
been neatly elevated by the blast of air. A great blue, foul
globule of air burst up into the open air. The maelstrom
swept through the steaming interior of the control room
as the bridge watch and lookouts raced for the ladder.
The gales of wind from fore and aft met and funneled
upward into the control room in one vast sweep that
seemed to carry the men upward. Bob's binoculars were
up over his head, held to his body only by the straps.
Papers, books, charts, and anything loose swirled upward
in one vast gush mingled with the acrid smoke of the
maneuvering room fire.

Bob staggered to his post. The fresh night air hit him
and his lungs filled with it as though they'd never get
enough. In five seconds he was completely sick over the
cigarette deck rail onto the streaming deck of the boat. He
didn't care. He was alive. He was breathing the God-
given air of the surface world. Bob raised his head, sick as
he was, for he had a duty to perform. The rain slanted
down wetting him to the skin, but it didn't make any difference, for his clothing was already soaked with his own
sweat.

163

There was a loud clang as the hydraulic mechanism opened the huge air-induction valve. The exhaust roar of a diesel broke the quiet of the empty, heaving waters. A small cloud of gray smoke poured from the exhaust. Three times, at rapid intervals, the process was repeated until four streams of exhaust vapor — two from each side of the dark hull — sputtered and spluttered as water attempted to flow back into the half-submerged pipes.

"Permission to start the turboblow, sir," said Ensign Tolliver.

"Permission granted," said the skipper.

"Permission to charge batteries, sir."

"Permission granted."

Grayfin began to pump air into the exhausted interior of the boat. The submarine began to move swiftly through the water with a high-pitched, screaming sound that could be heard above all the other noises. This was the low-pressure air blower, pumping atmospheric air into the ballast tanks, completing the emptying job that had been started submerged by the high-pressure air.

The rain sheeted down, forming an opaque screen. The radar antenna whirled steadily. It was doing its job now, for the radar had been fixed while *Grayfin* had suffered below. *Grayfin* burrowed deeper into the squall, making a respectable twelve knots while one of her diesels was fully occupied recharging an empty storage battery. *Grayfin* was running away, but only long enough to lick and heal her many wounds. She would be back.

Bob peered through the slanting rain. Once he thought he caught a glimpse of faint lights far astern, but he wasn't sure. Somewhere back there was Tawitawi with a Japanese tin can's crew congratulating themselves that they had sunk an American submarine.

There would be no rest for the crew of the *Grayfin*. Even as fresh air poured into the reeking hull the various details were hard at work plugging leaks, replacing wiring and piping, cleaning up the filthy mess on the decks, replacing shattered light bulbs, pumping out the bilges, blowing out the smoke and foul air, and sucking in the fresh night air to replace it.

At intervals, during Bob's watch, little groups of men would come up on the gently rolling deck and gulp in fresh air, only to dive below after a few moments to get their jobs done.

Grayfin bored on for long hours as the work went on. Once radar contact was made on several pips, identified tentatively as a small convoy, but *Grayfin* ignored them. She wasn't ready *yet*, but she would be. *She would be. . . .* This time there was no discontent among officers and crew. No longer did they have to remain targetless because of their orders.

She dived at dawn, batteries fully charged, air flasks full, with the interior smelling as fresh as it could, to come to rest at one hundred feet, far out of the lanes used and patrolled by enemy A/S vessels. Only the men necessary to attend certain functions remained on duty. The rest ate the best meal Blascovitz and his assistant could prepare, with seconds and thirds as a matter of course. Then it was sack time, for blessed sleep.

Grayfin rose dripping from the depths in the late afternoon and turned her bullnose back toward Tawitawi, but not directly toward the great anchorage. Those tin cans might still be there, not that *Grayfin* wasn't going to take a crack at them later, but right now she wanted to see what type of convoy activity was going on in the lanes approaching the anchorage.

Radar picked up a mess of pips, about ten miles from the submarine. *Grayfin* roared on at her full twenty knots, parting the smoothly rolling waters. Four sharp-eyed lookouts hung against the steel rings of their stations and probed the water surface and the darkening sky, and two of those lookouts knew they were going into action with a fleet submarine for the first time. This was different, very different from their service aboard a merchant craft in the Aleutians, and aboard a destroyer and PT in the Pacific.

Radar readings came in with more frequency, and sonar picked up the sound of many screws. Twelve ships moving *away* from Tawitawi at steady fifteen knots, fast time for a convoy.

"Convoy dead ahead, sir!" called out Red Kelly.

Grayfin slowed down her headlong rush. The speed was over. It was time to stalk the targets so temptingly displayed on the darkened surface of the sea. In the curious half-light of dusk, distance could be deceiving.

"Three destroyers. Nine merchant ships." This was the report from sonar. A moment later radar verified the sonarman's estimate.

"Maybe tankers," said Mack Davis. "They have some high-speed tankers. Fast time for a convoy. They don't want to waste any time around here, Skipper."

Tankers and destroyers were top-priority stuff, thought Bob, but three destroyers would be more than a mouthful for *Grayfin.* Still there was cold hate for the enemy in the crew of the boat, and possibly cold hate in the mechanical heart and brain of *Grayfin.* The last was difficult to tell. *Grayfin* had been hurt and hurt again and no one really knew if she had recovered. Time would tell.

The gap had closed to three miles and still *Grayfin*

continued to dog the fleeing convoy.

"Destroyer has turned in her tracks, sir!" reported radar. "Heading right at us, sir!"

"Stand by to dive! Lookouts below!" The klaxon blared. "Clear the bridge! Dive! Dive! Dive!"

Grayfin slid easily beneath the dark waters and in one minute she was below the surface leaving a froth of foam purling behind her. The bell clanged for battle stations.

"Up periscope!" Commander Currie studied the on-coming tin can. "Down periscope!"

The stalking began in tense and deadly earnest. This was the moment for which eight officers and seventy-five enlisted men had been trained and retrained.

"Up periscope!"

Bearings and data were fed into the TDC, the Torpedo Data Computer, a device for deriving a torpedo fire-control solution from data fed into it concerning the target's course, range, and speed. This would be combined with data on the submarine's course and speed, and the speed of the torpedo itself.

"Down periscope!"

"She's echo-ranging, sir!" reported sonar.

Grayfin moved as silently as possible through the depths. She twisted and turned away from the hunting tin can. Meanwhile the convoy kept racing on.

"Up periscope!" A moment or two of tension. "Down periscope! After room make ready the after tubes! Open outer doors in after room! Up periscope!" Commander Currie wet his dry lips as he peered through the periscope. "Mark!" he said. Range and bearings were instantly read off to be fed into the hungry, whirring TDC. "Stand by to fire . . . steady now . . . *steady!* Fire Seven! Fire Eight! Fire Nine! Fire Ten!" Four torpedoes hissed from the stern stingers of *Grayfin*. The submarine shuddered as the weight left her. The difference in weight was instantly compensated for by the diving officer. Men looked at one another or at their watches, mentally ticking off the seconds of the run.

A dull thud came through the depths, followed by another and another. The score was three out of four! Top-hole shooting! Three thunderous explosions followed the impact of the three fish.

"The first fish hit her bow," said Commander Currie. "The second hit just below her bridge. Third hit her amidships. I estimate her as a 1,500-ton destroyer of the *Minatsuki*-class. She's breaking in half."

The breaking-up noises came clearly through the water to *Grayfin,* and it was hard to hear them because of the sustained cheering of the delirious members of *Grayfin's* patient crew.

"Take a look, Mack," said the skipper.

The exec peered through the eyepieces. "The stern is rising," he said. "Her screws are still turning. The bow is gone. She's on fire. You can see the crew abandoning ship." He was very quiet for a moment. "Good Lord," he said softly, "she's gone. She's completely gone. Nothing left but floating debris, an oil slick, and swimming men." His voice died away.

Grayfin broke the surface and sped past the pitiful remnants of a proud destroyer of his Imperial Japanese Majesty's Navy. There was no time to pick up survivors, nor would they have accepted being saved. The floundering men looked away as *Grayfin* sped on, her diesels roaring, her speed to twenty knots. There were still eleven enemy ships against the dark horizon. Bob raised his glasses. He lowered them and listened to the exhausts and the muted roaring of the diesels. They sounded different.

Red Kelly looked at Bob out of the corner of his eye. "Yes," he said quietly. "They *do* sound different. The old girl has tasted first real blood for this patrol. She's *snarling*, Mac. Listen to her!"

There was no doubt about it. Bob nodded. He listened to the roaring of the submarine as she closed the convoy. She had five knots on them. The destroyers could do thirty to thirty-five knots, but the convoy ships couldn't. The destroyers were tied to the slower ships.

"Destroyer turning, sir!" said radar. "She's doing the same thing! Heading back! Fast!"

Bob could see the dim shape of the oncoming can and the V-shaped lather of luminous spray as her sharp bows cleaved the water at thirty knots, but this lad was sharper than the skipper of the sunk destroyer. He zigzagged, throwing the speeding craft from side to side as he approached.

"Lookouts below! Clear the bridge! Pull the plug!" came the command.

Grayfin slid below and twisted away from the oncoming tin can. She rose to periscope depth. Commander Currie studied the can. "Zigzagging all over the barnyard," he said thoughtfully.

The menacing sound of the screws came and went above the submarine as she sank below periscope depth. *Schir-schir-schir-schir* sounded throughout the hull of the boat.

"Up periscope! Down periscope! Forward room make ready the bow tubes! Open outer doors! Up periscope! *Mark!*"

The TDC absorbed the data, humming quietly to itself while dial needles spun about.

"Here she comes! Mark! Stand by to fire! Fire One! Fire Two! Fire Three! Fire Four!"

The submarine shuddered with the shock of releasing the four steel fish. Every man counted to himself, but time ticked past with no welcome impact thuds.

"She swerved at the last possible second," said the skipper. "It's our turn again. Down periscope! Take her deep! Rig for depth charges! Rig for silent running!"

Grayfin slanted downhill. Something clicked and then the first ash can exploded, followed quickly by another and another. *Grayfin* shuddered convulsively as each depth charge let go with 230 pounds of explosives. The depth gauge needle sank lower and lower. The sound of the screws came and went and now and then the Japanese skipper dumped a can or two to let *Grayfin* know he was still alert. An hour went by and then the screws faded away.

"Secure from battle stations," came the command.

The convoy was well out of harm's way by now and even so, the skipper of the destroyer that had just depth-charged them was no amateur like the skipper of the one that had been sunk. He knew his business. *Grayfin* had done well. Few submarines had ever sunk destroyers. There was other game off Tawitawi, and *Grayfin* had expended only eight torpedoes. Cheap at many times the price.

They surfaced and raced toward Tawitawi in the darkness before the rising of the moon.

14

Moonlight flecked the dark waters off Tawitawi, while here and there, through the overcast of clouds, came the full light of the moon to silver the water. Bright as it was, there were great patches of darker areas where visibility was tricky.

A scabrous-looking black shark of a hull crept through the waters, moving at slow speed. Radar felt through the night, and sonar felt through the dark waters. Constant reports came up to the cramped little bridge to the skipper. Now and then the diesels were stopped and the boat drifted.

" Contact, sir! " came the radar report. " Two pips! Destroyers possibly! Bearing two-two-oh. Range twenty thousand yards! "

Grayfin dived swiftly at the command and leveled off at periscope depth. " Battle stations torpedo! " came the command. The bell clanged.

The cans were echo-ranging. They might be the pair that had given *Grayfin* such a hard time before. *Grayfin* rose to take a quick look-see, then sank again.

Pinggg . . . pinggg . . . pinggg sounded through sonar.

It was a game of cat and mouse as the submarine and the two hunting destroyers felt for each other like blind wrestlers waiting for a sign of weakness in their opponent. Depth charges against torpedoes. Speed against stalking skill.

" Fast screws! Starboard beam! " reported sonar.

Pinggg . . . *pinggg* . . . *pinggg* . . . *poing* . . . *poing* . . . *poingg* . . . *poingg* . . . *poinggg* . . . *poinggg* . . . *poinggg* . . . The tin can was making contact on *Grayfin*. The screws of the second one had faded away.

The bow angle was zero now. The tin can was coming steadily on. The echo-ranging was coming with more frequency. Short-range stuff.

" Up periscope! Down periscope! She's spotted the scope," said the skipper. " Make ready the bow tubes! Open outer doors! Stand by! Steady . . . steady . . . *steady* . . . Fire One! Fire Two! Fire Three! " Three tin fish hissed from the tubes, range fifteen hundred yards, gyro angles near zero — a real " down the throat " shot, directly from the bows of the submarine toward the lean bows of the oncoming destroyer.

" Fast screws closing in, port beam! " reported sonar.

" All ahead, full left rudder! Take her deep! " snapped the skipper.

Grayfin nosed down deeply. The depth gauge marked eighty feet, fifty-five seconds after the first torpedo had hissed from the tube, when the first blast came, followed by another. " We're diving below her," said Currie, matter-of-factly. " I hope we're moving faster than she's sinking."

The explosion came with stunning force and it was far worse than any depth-charging *Grayfin* had experienced. She shuddered and shivered, pitched and rolled, throwing men about like dice in a cup. Bulbs jolted out of their sockets and rained glass down on the shrinking crew. A

172

deafening series of explosions penetrated to the diving submarine.

"Her boilers or magazines, maybe both, have let go," said Chief Daly. "I heard this happen before." He grinned weakly. "Good thing for *Grayfin* that ship explosions blast upward instead of downward or we'd be heading for Davy Jones's locker."

Click . . . WHAM! Click . . . WHAM! Click . . . WHAM! . . . Click . . . WHAM! Explosion after explosion blasted water at *Grayfin*.

"The other can is depth-charging us," said Gary.

Chief Daly shook his head. "Those are the depth charges letting go on her own decks as she sinks. They should have been disarmed, but they didn't have time. Those charges will kill every man in the water."

An instrument flew from a bulkhead and clanged on the deck. A pipe snapped loose and struck like a rattlesnake at Slim Polk. He went down unconscious with blood streaming from his face.

Gradually the breaking-up noises subsided as the can sank deeper and deeper and the last of her depth charges let go. *Grayfin* crept away. The sound of distant echo-ranging came through the hull.

"Two cans," said Mack Davis. "That's a record! Wait until we get back to base!"

Commander Currie looked at him. "You're not thinking of quitting now, Mack?" he said in mock surprise.

The big exec smiled sheepishly. "Not exactly. I figured we earned our pay so far."

"We've got plenty of fish left, Mack."

Grayfin surfaced two hours after she had sunk the second destroyer. The moon was still fully up. Radar made contact with three pips. Sonar picked up high-speed screws moving at right angles to the course of the submarine. *Grayfin* surged on through the moonlight, careless of discovery. There was a confidence in the old girl now. This was to be her day and none could deny it to her. She dived when within two miles of the three ships.

"Battle stations submerged!" The bong-bong-bong of the alarm sounded throughout the submarine.

"Up periscope!" Commander Currie rode it up and began to study this new game. "A destroyer, a smaller A/S vessel and . . ." His voice died away and he whistled softly. "A tanker! A big one! Twelve thousand tons at least and down to her plimsolls with oil and gas. Take a gander, Mack."

The exec peered through the eyepieces and whistled softly as the skipper had done. "That tin can is a good-sized one too! I make her to be *Hayanami*-class, say about the size of our *Fletcher*-class. Twenty-one hundred tons at least, Skipper." He studied the unsuspecting target. "That A/S vessel is a frigate type. About twelve hundred tons at least."

The skipper took over the scope and guided *Grayfin* by his quiet commands. This was his show. Even *Grayfin* depended on him. Fifteen hundred tons of the most complex machinery in the Navy, three hundred and seven feet long, driven by four diesel engines with a combined thrust of seventy-two-hundred horsepower manned by eight officers and seventy-four specialists, with ten torpedo tubes ready for action. It was up to the one man to guide and control this fighting machine against a tanker, a destroyer, and a frigate — all vital to the Japanese Navy and the war in general. *Grayfin* still had eleven fish to fire from her stingers.

"The destroyer has turned away," he said. "Angling

away from the tanker. Down periscope."

Grayfin moved through the water at her full underwater speed of ten knots, for which her batteries were good for one hour. She dived deeply and turned away and then worked her way up on the far side of the little group of ships. A periscope look-see showed the destroyer on the far side, at least two miles from the tanker that forged along convoyed by the smaller frigate.

Mack Davis looked up from a ship identification book. "That tanker is almost identical to the *Kachisan Maru*, Skipper. You were a little short on your tonnage. She's closer to fifteen thousand tons than twelve thousand."

"What's her keel depth?"

"Thirty feet loaded."

"Deep . . . deep. Top speed?"

"Fifteen knots."

"She's making close to that now. She's in a hurry to get to Tawitawi. The A/S vessel has dropped behind her and is crossing over toward us. Down scope! Rig for silent running! Dive to eighty feet!"

Grayfin slid deeper and deeper, but there was no sound of echo-ranging. Sonar picked up her screws steadily approaching the area over the submarine, and the savage chow - chow - chow - chow - CHOW - CHOW - CHOW - CHOW of the whirling blades passed right over the *Grayfin*. The sounds of the screws faded away.

"Periscope depth!" *Grayfin* rose slowly upward to sixty feet. "Up periscope!" The periscope whined up out of its well, ridden up by the skipper. "Forward room make ready the bow tubes! Open outer doors!" The TDC began to whir thoughtfully to itself. "Angle on the bow eighty degrees starboard! Stand by to mark the range! *Mark!*"

"Two-eight-oh-oh!" snapped the enlisted man.

" Come right two degrees! "

The deck tilted a little. The TDC whirred.

" Torpedoes ready for firing, sir! "

" Fire One! Fire Two! Fire Three! Fire Four! " came the command.

The submarine shuddered and nearly broached as twelve thousand pounds of metal fish sped from the tubes. Seconds ticked past. Men looked at each other out of the corners of their eyes. There were two faint explosions. Then came a dull thud.

" Two prematures. One miss," said the skipper.

" High-speed screws approaching from starboard beam," reported sonar.

" I see him," said the skipper. " Down periscope! Dive to one hundred feet! Full left rudder! Rig for silent running! "

The *Grayfin* dived and twisted away from the oncoming A/S vessel. The sound of the screws went right over the sinking submarine and passed on, fading away. " Lousy echo-ranging on that tub," said the skipper.

It was very quiet in the boat.

" You said two prematures and one miss, Skipper," said Lieutenant Olson. " That leaves one fish unaccounted for."

The skipper nodded. " Beats me," he said.

" There was a dull, thudding noise," said Ensign Tolliver.

They all looked at each other. " You don't suppose? " said Lieutenant Olson.

Mack Davis nodded. " A hit without an explosion."

" Turn on the sonar speaker, Scarlotti," said the skipper.

There was an intermingling of sounds. Scarlotti looked up. " The A/S boy is heading back toward the tanker. I can still pick up the tin can's screws. She's coming in fast too." He closed his eyes. "There's something missing," he added. "The third set of screws! The tanker has stopped moving!"

"Dead in the water," said the skipper. "That fourth fish didn't explode, but it damaged the tanker somehow."

It was tensely silent throughout the boat. The faint *thum - thum - thum - thum - thum - thum - thum - thum - thum - thum* of the screws of the tin can and the A/S vessel came through the sonar gear. It hadn't been the skipper's fault that two of the fish had been prematures. If they had gone on to the tanker, they might have flamed her. Each man did a little simple arithmetic in his mind. They had expended fifteen torpedoes. There were seven left. Tubes Four, Five, Six in the bow were still loaded, and all four after tubes, Seven, Eight, Nine, and Ten were loaded. There were no reserve torpedoes. There were still three enemy vessels up on that moonlit sea.

"Periscope depth!" ordered Commander Currie.

Grayfin rose obediently. The periscope whirred up out of its tube. "The tanker is dead in the water," said the skipper. He looked away from the eyepieces. One could almost see the thought processes of his mind depicted on his sweat-damp face. What was more important? The dead tanker or the two escort vessels? How should they be approached? Should he use bow or stern tubes?

He peered through the eyepieces again. "After room make ready the after tubes! Open outer doors!" He studied the problem. "Moon is almost gone," he said.

It was very quiet in the boat except for the gurgling of the tanks as the diving officer kept the *Grayfin* at periscope level. The big steel fish moved without fuss through the water. "Mark," said the skipper. Range and bearings were

177

read off to be fed into the TDC. " Stand by to fire! Steady . . . steady . . . *steady!* Fire Seven! Fire Eight! Fire Nine! Fire Ten! " *Grayfin* shuddered convulsively as four deadly missiles hissed from the tubes and plunged through the water. Seconds ticked past. WHUMPH! WHUMPH! WHUMPH! WHUMPH! There was no doubt about the success of the four torpedoes. Four direct hits in vital places.

Commander Currie stared fascinated through the periscope.

" High-speed screws approaching from port beam! " reported the sonarman.

The skipper did not move. " She's blown up completely," he said in awe. " The whole sea is alight."

" Sir! " said Scarlotti. " Listen! " He switched on the sonar speaker and the roaring of the screws filled the submarine.

Currie awoke as though from a trance. " Dive to one hundred feet! Rig for silent running! Full right rudder! "

They all knew he was going to use the same tactics. Dive under the sinking tanker. The screws sounded savagely like trains running over a trestle. *Chow-chow-chow-chow-chow-CHOW-CHOW-CHOW-CHOW-CHOW!*

They could hear the tanker breaking up, a series of cracking, shattering, snapping noises magnified by the carrying powers of the water. Eyes flicked upward as each man performed his duty. The water was filled with a cacophony of noises, overlaid one upon another, intermingled and intertwined, until the impression was indescribable. The sound grew louder and louder. Something struck *Grayfin*, and the sound echoed and reechoed throughout the submarine. Something exploded with shocking violence beneath the water. Then the noises fell

178

astern. Deeper and deeper burrowed *Grayfin* until she was far away from the two angry, buzzing hornets on the surface. Three tin fish still nestled in the bow tubes of *Grayfin*. They were the last in the locker, and there were still two targets on the surface.

"Stand by to surface! Battle stations surface!" The klaxon broke the quiet in the submarine. *Grayfin* tilted upward out of the depths. She broke water and almost instantly the bridge watch and the lookouts were at their posts. Far off across the dark heaving waters, lighted faintly by the dying moon, could be seen the faint, dark shapes of the two Japanese escort vessels. They had already failed in their job and now they were feeling about for *Grayfin* for revenge.

Grayfin was low in the water, black-painted, scabbed with rust and leprous with salt, and with nothing to reflect light. She skulked in the darker areas caused by overhanging clouds. Far beyond the two escort vessels could be seen the faint lights of Tawitawi.

The smaller vessel moved away from the destroyer. The destroyer turned toward *Grayfin*. She moved rather slowly, zigzagging from side to side, and the sound of her echoranging came faintly to *Grayfin*.

"Radar," said the skipper, "range me that can."

"Three thousand yards, sir," came the prompt response.

Almost as though the destroyer had heard, it turned more to the unseen *Grayfin*. The tin can commenced weaving and increased its speed. It must have detected the submarine. *Grayfin* dived to periscope depth and kept on toward the oncoming ship. The sonarman on *Grayfin* trained his gear from side to side to pick up all sectors. Fast screws bearing zero-nine-zero, short-scale pinging.

179

That meant only one thing. The smaller vessel had moved in too.

"One thousand yards," said the skipper calmly. "Stand by forward! Stand by Four! Angle on the bow, ten port, increasing! He's starting to swing back! Angle on the bow, twenty port! Bearing — mark! Stand by!"

The TDC was instantly checked and observed that the generated target bearing on the TDC was exactly the same as the periscope bearing. Mack Davis looked up. "Set," he said.

"Fire Four!" barked the skipper.

The *Grayfin* shuddered. "Right full rudder! All ahead full!" commanded the skipper. "He didn't complete his full swing!"

There was no sound from the lone tin fish as it sped harmlessly past the oncoming destroyer. *Grayfin* plunged for the depths. She knew what was coming. She was at seventy feet when the first depth charge let go, but it was too far away to do any damage. Deeper and deeper she went until the sound of the depth charges came from afar off. She hung at one hundred and fifty feet about the time the last depth charge exploded.

An hour drifted slowly past, then two, with the faint sound of echo-ranging coming through the depths. The moon would be gone by now and the surface would be dark. The Japanese craft would be moving about up there in the thick darkness still feeling for *Grayfin*. Two targets on the surface and two torpedoes left in the forward tubes. *Grayfin* could go home. She had sunk two destroyers and a tanker. There would be no shame in going home.

"It will be daylight in a couple of hours," said Mack Davis.

There was no answer from the skipper.

"They'll have a mess of A/S vessels out at dawn," said Tom Olson.

"With plane coverage," said Ensign Tolliver.

Currie looked at them. "You sound as though you want to go home," he said.

"Not me," said Mack Davis. "With two fish left?"

"It was a matter of time, Skipper," said Tom Olson.

"Periscope depth," commanded the officer.

Grayfin surged eagerly upward. She wasn't through fighting as long as she had two torpedoes left.

"Dark as the inside of a boot," said the skipper.

"High-speed screws bearing three-three-oh!" reported sonar.

"More than one?" said the skipper.

"Just one, sir."

"Maybe one of the boys went home," said Mack Davis.

The skipper turned the periscope. "Not likely," he said. "He's probably sitting up there echo-ranging for us. Let's rise and get the radar mast out of the drink."

Radar reported two pips, as Commander Currie had suspected. The surface of the sea was dark. Somewhere up there, unseen by the periscope but detected by radar and sonar, the two vessels worked together.

"Down periscope," said the skipper as he slapped the training handles upward. He shoved back his hat and wiped the sweat from his face. "Not much choice," he said. "I can't afford to take one shot at each of them. It will have to be two fish for one of them. We can get a good shot at that smaller boat. He passed right over us and all around us and never got a good sound contact. That can is different. He's alert. Maybe we're playing our luck too far by thinking about taking on the can."

"*Who* was thinking of taking on the can?" murmured

181

Lieutenant Gamble, the torpedo officer.

"They're moving together," said Scarlotti.

"Rise to radar depth," said Commander Currie.

The mast cleared the dark waters. Bader studied his screen. "Scarlotti is right," he said quietly. "They're very close."

"Both of them have slowed down," said the sonarman.

"Give me a turn count," said the skipper.

Scarlotti listened intently. "Turn count about ten knots," he announced.

"Up periscope," said the skipper. He rode it up and studied the dark sea above the slowly moving submarine. "I can barely make them out," he said. "Close together."

"They're turning away again," said radar.

Grayfin's speed was increased to ten knots, the best she could do below the surface, and every man aboard was positive those keen-eyed Japanese lookouts, with their excellent night glasses, could pick up the thread of foam rippling back from the periscope and radar mast.

"Dawn is coming along," said the executive officer.

"We've still got time," said the skipper.

Minutes ticked past as *Grayfin* maneuvered. Gary padded up to Bob and handed him a sandwich. Bob bit into it, positive the enemy could hear his teeth biting through.

Commander Currie made an observation every thirty seconds or so. The periscope was in almost continual motion, up and down, up and down. Sweat dripped from the skipper's face and from the ends of his fingers where they gripped the training handles. Everything else in the conning tower was stock-still, as though time had ceased to function, except for the range counters on the TDC which steadily indicated the range.

The range had dwindled to three thousand yards. The radar screen showed the two pips side by side, moving slowly. " He's heading directly across our bows," said the skipper. " The smaller vessel is dropping behind."

The range dials on the TDC reached fifteen hundred yards. Target speed was twelve knots. Angle on the bow starboard seventy-five. Bearing 335.

" Stand by forward! Bearing! Mark! Fire Five! Fire Six! " *Grayfin* lurched as the heavy torpedoes sped from the tubes. Every man aboard *Grayfin* mentally ticked off the seconds. They had missed. It was taking too long. They had lost both torpedoes. These thoughts raced through every man's mind.

Thud . . . slam . . . WHOOOOM! . . . thud . . . slam . . . WHOOOOM!

Cheers echoed through the submarine The skipper had done it again! Two hits on the tin can!

The commander peered through the periscope.

"Watch out for the A/S craft! " said Mack Davis. He was out of order and he knew it, but he didn't want the boat to be risked after such a record.

The skipper looked up from the eyepieces. " Sonar," he said, " switch on the speaker."

Scarlotti flipped the switch. Breaking-up noises came through the speaker, a crackling, grinding, snapping, and roaring confusion.

" No screws," said the skipper.

" No screws," said Scarlotti.

No one spoke. Only *Grayfin* made mechanical noises as she was kept at periscope depth.

" Take a look-see, Mack," said the skipper.

The big exec peered through the periscope eyepieces. He whistled sharply. " A doubleheader! " he said.

183

Each officer in turn peered through the scope. Then it was the turn of some of the enlisted men.

"Down scope," commanded the skipper. "Stand by to surface!"

Grayfin roared up to the surface and the hatch was flung open. Cool air flowed into the submarine. Bob reached his post and came up through the lookout ring before he glanced out across the dark waters. A dull explosion occurred beneath the surface and a great bubble burst high in the air scattering debris across the surface.

There wasn't a sound from any of the men watching the scene. Steam and smoke hung over the gently heaving waters like a shroud. A lighted buoy bobbed on the waters shedding an uneven glow.

One after another the crewmen of the *Grayfin* came up on the deck and looked silently at the scene. It was eerie up there, eerie and deathly quiet. The water washed in and out of the freeing ports. It was as quiet as the grave after the crashing hell of destruction that had sent both Japanese vessels to the bottom in a matter of minutes.

No one spoke, but eyes flicked toward the impassive face of the skipper. With two torpedoes he had managed to sink two dangerous, skillful enemy vessels, any one of which was possibly more than a match for the average submarine.

The engine room annunciators tinkled. The diesels roared into life at rapid intervals, a cloud of smoke arose from the exhaust pipes. *Grayfin* turned away from the silent scene of destruction.

Commander Currie shoved back his hat and looked back at that lonely flare still bobbing up and down on the empty waters. *Grayfin* had fulfilled her mission. She had sunk two A/S vessels earlier and now three destroyers, one A/S vessel and a big tanker, and had scouted the anchorage at Tawitawi. He looked about at his bridge watch and up at the lookouts. " Gentlemen," he said, " let's head for the barn! All ahead, standard! " The annunciators tinkled and *Grayfin* surged along.

Bob and Gary sat quietly in the crew's messroom listening to the conversation of the other men. They were not part of the crew of this fighting submarine, but they had served with her and of that they could be proud.

Baldy looked up from an ancient magazine. " Luck," he said. " We missed the tin can with the second torpedo and hit the A/S. Luck I calls it! "

Red Kelly looked at him. " Luck? Why, you knothead! Skipper planned it all along that way! "

" How do you know? How will any of us know? " demanded the skeptical motormac.

Blascovitz jerked a thumb. " There he is, Baldy," he said. " You can ask him."

All eyes turned to see the skipper. Baldy flushed.

" Go on, Baldy," said Slim Polk.

Baldy stood up. " I was just wondering, sir," he said. " No offense, sir, but did you *plan* it that way? "

Commander Currie smiled. " Well now, gentlemen," he said, " that's between me and *Grayfin*, don't you think? Let's leave it that way." He walked aft to the forward engine room.

Gary tilted his head and half closed his eyes. " Listen to her, fellows," he said softly. " I'll swear the old girl is purring like a kitten."

It was so. She was on her way back to base. A bit rusty and a bit battered, but her torpedoes were all gone. There would be a broom lashed to her masthead, and a string of meatball flags fluttering in the Australian wind when she came slowly into port. No one would notice her rust and scars. They'd be watching the broom that signified she had swept the waters off Tawitawi and they could count the meatball flags. It was all down in the log; *the log of the Grayfin.*

Bibliography

Beach, Commander Edward L., *Submarine!* Signet Books, 1957.

Chambliss, William C., *The Silent Service*. Signet Books, 1959.

Grider, George and Sims, Lydel, *War Fish*. Little, Brown and Company, 1958.

Morison, Samuel Eliot, *History of United States Naval Operations in World War II*, Vol. VII, *Aleutians, Gilberts and Marshalls, June 1942–April 1944*. Little, Brown and Company, 1961.

Roscoe, Theodore, *United States Submarine Operations in World War II*. U.S. Naval Institute, 1949.

Rush, Captain, C. W., and others, *The Complete Book of Submarines*, rev. ed. Random House, Inc., 1963.

Sterling, Forest J., *Wake of the Wahoo*. Chilton Company, 1960.

Trumbull, Robert, *Silversides*. Henry Holt & Co., 1945.

Weller, George, *The Story of Submarines*. Random House, Inc., 1962.

Biography of Gordon D. Shirreffs

Gordon D. Shirreffs was born in Chicago, Illinois, where he attended grammar school and high school. While in high school he was active in R.O.T.C., track, wrestling, and rifle-shooting. After leaving high school, he worked at various jobs, his best memories being of two summer seasons spent as a hand on a fifty-foot sailing ketch cruising the Great Lakes. Later he enlisted in the Illinois National Guard and started work at the Union Tank Car Company of Chicago. At night he studied at Northwestern University.

In September, 1940, he was called to active military service as a sergeant in the antiaircraft artillery. He was promoted to second lieutenant in January, 1941. During the war years he served in Alaska and throughout the Aleutian campaign, later serving as a transport commander on a Norwegian ship, the *Fridtjof Nansen,* in Mediterranean waters. He was honorably discharged in December, 1945, with the rank of captain. He went back to work at the Union Tank Car Company and reentered Northwestern University, Medill School of Journalism, to study professional fiction-writing. From 1946 until 1952 he worked as a salesman, booking agent, and demonstrator. He also had short stories published in boys' magazines and in adventure magazines.

Mr. Shirreffs moved to California in 1952, and bought a home in Granada Hills in the San Fernando Valley, where he took up full-time professional writing. At the present time he has sold over two hundred short stories, *novelas* and novelettes, fifty-five full-length books, seventeen in the juvenile category, two movies, *The Lonesome Trail* and *Oregon Passage, The Galvanized Yankee* on *Playhouse 90*, based on his book *Massacre Creek*, and two other television plays. Books and stories have been printed in Canada, Australia, the United Kingdom, Denmark, Finland, Germany, Holland, Spain, France, Norway, Sweden, and Italy. Three of his boys' stories have been printed in Braille. Others have appeared in *The Boys Life Book of Scout Stories, Boys Life Treasury, Teen-Age Frontier Stories, Young in the Saddle,* and in *Frontiers to Explore, Teacher's Edition.*

His hobbies are Western and Civil War history, archery, rifle and pistol markmanship, and modelmaking, and he has acted as technical adviser and archer in movies. One of his most interesting hobbies is playing the tenor drum in the San Fernando–Burbank Fire Department Bagpipe Band. He is an active member of the Veterans of Foreign Wars.

He and his wife have a daughter, Carole Alice, and a son, Brian Allen.

190